My Name

Is Della

And I'm Dead

Erik Volk

Cover design by Full Circle Endeavors.

ISBN-13: 978-1514710975

ISBN-10: 1514710978

For Phil,
with love and gratitude.

And with thanks to Ellen
for her advice and friendship.

One

My name is Della and I'm dead. Della Marie Hampton to be exact. The day I died may have been the first day I truly appreciated life. Death was not exactly what I expected and definitely not anything like what they preached in church. My experiences weren't much like what my "psychic" friends had predicted, and quite a bit different from all the stories on the TV talk shows from people who allegedly had "died" and lived to talk about it. I can't necessarily tell you what will happen to you after you kick the bucket, but I can tell you what happened to me and that my friends, is quite the story.

To be honest, I had never really thought a great deal about death. At least, I never thought about it anymore than the average person did. However, I never really thought about life much either. I fell into the pattern that so many of us do when you hit your forties. Life became a seemingly endless cycle of sleep, work, eat, and repeat with the occasional get-togethers with friends and the even more occasional sprinkling of sex and romance.

My life was good if uneventful. I was approaching forty-three at the time of my demise and was a project manager for a medium sized insurance company. This type of job certainly wasn't the dream career I had hoped for when I was young and chock-full of hopes and dreams. When I was in my early twenties and fresh out of Boston College, I was certain I was going to be a journalist, writing stories from around the globe and making my indelible mark on the world.

By the time I was twenty-four, I discovered that my passion for journalism was overshadowed by the sad realization that the best job I could seemingly get was writing obituaries for a newspaper in East Armpit Texas, for less than I made as a waitress at McAllister's Pub & Grille. So instead, I took a job at an insurance company as a customer service representative, telling myself that this was a temporary detour on my intended path to fame and glory.

I ended up working at five different insurance companies during my human existence in a variety of increasingly responsible roles, and ultimately landed a position as a project manager at Arkville Insurance Company in the humble metropolis of Hartford, Connecticut at the age of thirty-seven. I felt at home in Hartford. At the time of my demise, the city of Hartford and I had a lot in common. We were both looking a little bit older, getting a little gray around the edges and didn't like to take shit from anybody.

I thought my job was sufficiently boring but also thought it paid sufficiently well. Since I had no children, it was fairly easy for me to save up the funds to pay for a lovely town home in the funky neighborhood of West Hartford as well as to satisfy my gourmet cheese fetish and take the occasional semi-luxurious vacation. As much as I groaned at the thought of having to go into the office each Monday morning, in retrospect, I guess I really did like my job.

As I alluded to earlier, romance did not play a huge part in my life. Well, there had been a few romantic relationships with men over the years. However, none of them really worked out.

In my younger days, I dreamed of finding my soul mate. He would be a handsome man who would make love to me nightly, make me the center of his universe and shower me with gifts and love each day of our blissful existence together. However, every year I got older, I found that the reality more often than not, was men became possessive, childish and extremely irritating. In reality, I am sure I was not the glamourous trophy girlfriend so many men I dated hoped for either. The thought of someone messing up my bathroom, eating my ice cream or forcing me to watch televised sports made it clear that any possible romance could not include us sharing our living space.

After my fortieth birthday, I decided that I could fare much better by myself, with the occasional romp in the sheets with men with whom I had no plans of pursuing long-term relationships. I had a brief, singular foray with lesbianism with my friend Amanda after many cocktails, watching several episodes of a lesbian soap opera and her complimenting me continuously. When you are insecure like me, endless compliments can entice you to explore unchartered territories. However, I can definitely say that the lesbian thing was not for me. At the start of the night's events, it was great to have someone focused on providing me pleasure but I can tell you when it was my turn to return the favor, the whole affair just left a bad taste in my mouth. I was all for gay rights but I was clearly and inextricably, heterosexual. Maybe that's revealing a little too much...but what do I care? I'm dead!

The one steady male presence in my life was my dog Barry, named after the infamous crooner Barry Manilow. Barry Manilow's heartfelt songs paired with a cold glass of Chardonnay helped me through some difficult times in my life. My dog Barry also provided me great comfort, perhaps substituting in a way for my lack of romance. He was a cute little Boston Terrier who always seemed to know when a happy greeting full of sloppy kisses was in order, or when his quiet presence on my lap staring at me with his soulful eyes was more appropriate.

I seldom saw my family during the latter part of my life either. My dad, Barney, had died when I was in my late twenties from liver cancer that had quickly appeared, spread through his body like wildfire, and killed him within a month. My mother Helen, who was always a quiet woman, came out of her shell with a vengeance after my father's death. She became a whirlwind of activity, immersed herself in the subculture of yoga, would eat only organic foods and eventually at the age of sixty-nine, moved to a community outside of Orlando Florida, made up of similar elderly women (and some men) who reviled in the delight of being deliciously strange. Anyone who knew my mother during her child-rearing years would likely not even recognize the new somewhat extroverted woman she had become.

My mother was a fixture in the Orlando community theater circuit and had also started a small side business selling handmade sun hats which she sold in various boutiques throughout Central and Southern Florida. At the age of seventy-one, she married a guy twenty years her junior, named Kellin, who was inclined to utter strange phrases such as "your aura is emanating a

5

beautiful color blue today" and "any child who was brought forth from the powerful womb of your mother is welcome in my heart." Needless to say, I did not feel inclined to visit that commune of New Age bullshit too often.

I had one brother Daniel who lived not too far away in Newport, Rhode Island. He was three years my junior. Although we had been close when we were growing up and now only lived about an hour and a half apart, we did not see each other as much as one might expect. Daniel was an executive who worked for a large defense contractor and although he explained to me on many occasions the types of projects he worked on, I still have no clue exactly what he did.

Daniel was married to Janet. Janet was one of those women who was seemingly perfect, smart, successful, intelligent and beautiful. She was the type of person who made you sick to your stomach because you felt so inferior, and then made you sicker for thinking such awful thoughts about someone who seemed to be so damn nice.

They had one child, Jason, who had the perfect mixture of his father's brilliance and his mother's sweetness. Selfish as I was, Rhode Island always seemed just a little far away despite their continual invitations to stay at their palatial beach home in Newport. When it came down to whether I wanted to take a week's vacation with some of my girlfriends in Mexico or spend a week in Rhode Island with Daniel and his perfect family, Mexico usually won out.

I remember the last time I visited my brother's family and Janet greeted me at the door. She was dressed like a Donna Karan model in meticulously tailored clothes and I was in jeans and a T-Shirt with a faded Hartford Arts Festival logo on it. I had pulled my hair back into a makeshift ponytail using a rubber band I had found in my purse. I will never forget how insecure and frumpy I felt on that last visit. I was like a Walmart shopper who mistakenly stepped into a Rodeo Drive shop.

On that last visit, she had asked me to join her on a trip to a psychic she had been seeing. "Della, you won't believe how accurate her readings are. She managed to contact my mother and told me things she could not possibly have known." The prospect of her seeing a psychic seemed to me to be quite outside of Janet's normal character. Everything in Janet's life seemed to be known in advance, carefully planned, carefully organized and tied up with a handmade bow.

"Della..." she had told me, "You really should come. There could be exciting things planned in your future.

Who knows? Romance could be lurking right around the corner."

I resented her insinuation that my life wasn't exciting. I mean, truth be told, it really wasn't but I still resented the insinuation. And as far as romance "lurking right around the corner," I didn't need a psychic to predict that. My creepy neighbor Byron was just around the corner, one town house away, and he certainly always had romance on his mind. "Lurking" was definitely a good descriptor for Byron. As I had previously mentioned, I had all but sworn off men anyway and certainly was not interested in romance with a balding, beer-bellied creep who had a habit of yelling across the parking lot "Looking gooooood... Dellllaaaa!" and could not seem to keep his ear hair under control.

Besides, I thought all that psychic stuff was a bunch of nonsense. I was quite sure that the psychics managed to glean information from their unsuspecting clients using some sort of clever psychological tricks. Also, just in case you are not aware, there is this thing called the Internet. Even if nothing came up when you Googled yourself, you can be sure there was plenty of stuff about you out there for anyone clever enough to find it. I, myself, had posted a little too much on Facebook in a lame and probably unconscious attempt to make my life seem more interesting. If I had known that death was imminent, I may have removed some of my errant Facebook postings. I did worry that my legacy might consist entirely of some embarrassing photos and hundreds of comments that reflected my lame attempts at humor. Granted, at the time they seemed cleverly funny, but they seemed somewhat sad and pathetic in retrospect.

There were women my age who led multi-million dollar corporations, published best-selling books and even ruled countries. I feared my final contributions to the world might consist solely of pictures of me in an ill-fitting swimsuit drinking margaritas, informing everyone what eighties pop star I looked most like and details about my successful side career as a Candy Crush master. But I digress…

During my visits, my brother Daniel and his son Jason normally remained immobile and quiet in front of the TV set, but Daniel encouraged Janet and me to spend as much time together as possible. "Della…you should go. It would be fun for you and Janet to have a girls' day out. Don't worry about us. We'll be just fine. You have your girls' time and we'll have our guys' time."

It always seemed to me that his motivation for Janet and me to spend time together was more reflective of his desire to relax in his own home than for me and Janet to become best friends. I could picture him with his feet propped up on the highly polished coffee table, drinking beer and eating potato chips while watching his favorite sports show on television. All of these activities were normally highly discouraged if not specifically prohibited in his house by Janet. Of course, she always expressed her disapproval in the most pleasant fashion but she always got her way in the end. Passive-aggressive? Table for one, please. And just to forewarn you, Janet would like that table set with a tablecloth and real linen napkins if you would not mind.

In the end, I decided against the psychic visit and joined Janet, somewhat hesitatingly, for a day of shopping. Shopping, or at least Janet's version of shopping, was not an activity that thrilled me. It was more likely to cause me to suffer from acute anxiety and self-consciousness if not outright depression.

Few of the stores that Janet frequented carried my size and those stores usually employed salespeople who treated me as if I was invisible or at the very least unworthy of their attention. Similarly, the stores where I liked to shop seemed to cause Janet great duress and bring her to the edge of what appeared to be petit mal seizures. Whenever I convinced her to join me at one of my chosen shopping venues, she would often go pale and utterly silent. Once when I dragged her by the arm into a thrift store, I thought she might break out in tears.

You must understand that Janet was not a woman who was interested in finding bargains, and she disliked anything not made from natural fibers or that may have possibly come in contact with polyester. She often explained to me that polyester was made from plastic, and that plastic leached toxins into your skin which could lead to cancer, anemia or any assortment of other diseases. She also found it incredulous that I would not only purchase, but actually wear, a skirt I found for $9.99 at Danny's Discount Dress Barn.

Some of the discount stores were just too much for her to deal with and she would sometimes insist on waiting in the car. And… because I am a caring person, I always left the window rolled down a bit for her. Luckily, we both shared a love of Chardonnay and would make several stops during the day to have a bite to eat and a little wine. Securing a small buzz always seemed to make us both feel a little more comfortable; me a little less self-conscious, and Janet a little less epileptic during these shopping expeditions.

Lastly, before I get to my actual death and lest you think my existence was one of complete solitude and loneliness, I was very fortunate to have an array of friends with whom I regularly spent time. A group of us met every couple of weeks for cocktails, dinner, gossip, karaoke, game nights, potlucks. movies and other social activities.

My closest friend was Penny. Penny had worked with me in my twenties and we had maintained a relationship through the ebbs and flows of our lives. She had been married and divorced three times and similar to me had seemingly given up on men and romance. She had pretty much decided that cocktails with girlfriends, chocolate and battery powered stimulation could fill whatever void not having a man might have created. Although there were years when we had not talked very much, she had relocated to Connecticut five years prior to my death and our friendship had flourished. I really loved Penny. She made me laugh and her no nonsense approach to life often would bring me back from bouts of self-inflicted depression when Barry Manilow and Chardonnay could not.

I have so many wonderful memories of Penny and the fun times we had spent together. One of my favorite memories was of a trip we had taken to South Beach in Miami. We spent our days lounging on the beaches or by the hotel pool reading, drinking fruity cocktails and people watching.

On one of our outings, we unexpectedly ventured upon a nude beach and amused ourselves immensely watching the various characters roaming the shoreline. It was my first and only visit to a nude beach. If you have never been to a nude beach, let me assure that you are more likely to see people that look more like your Aunt Mabel and Uncle Dexter, than Brad Pitt and Angelina Jolie.

Now, we were certainly not going to win any beauty contests ourselves, and perhaps really should have been less judgmental but we were also not parading up and down the beach, displaying our wares. Penny had started to assign names to some of the people who seemed to be continuously passing by and then supplemented them by drawing crude cartoonlike renderings of them on a notepad. These efforts sent us into endless hysterics. It was all I could do contain my laughter.

One particular couple she had dubbed Ballsy and Titsy McGee. This couple, who were substantially overweight and perhaps in their early fifties, insisted on continuously engaging in Frisbee, directly in our line of vision. I could not even look at Penny for fear that I would burst out in laughter at any moment. Then, before I knew what was happening, Penny had grabbed me by the hand and pulled me towards the McGee's announcing loudly,

"Can my friend and I join you? We would love to play!" Before I knew what was happening, we were fully involved in a quasi-nude game of Frisbee. Penny even, somehow, convinced a passerby to snap a photo of the four of us, with the McGee's consent, of course. Penny and I kept our swimsuits on the whole time but the photo remained a souvenir of one of my most memorable vacations with Penny and a testament to her unique personality. She had a personality that never ceased to make me smile.

I missed my Mom and brother, but it was Penny and my dog Barry whom I missed the most. Perhaps, I should have missed my family more, but when you are dead guilt does not play such a huge role. In the end, I realized, you can't pick your family but you can pick your friends, your pets and your Chardonnay.

Two

Before I talk about the day I died, let me assure you that I am not minimizing the effect of death on loved ones. It is surely traumatic for most people and I suspect it also was for my family and friends. However, I cannot tell you how others reacted to my death, but only what I remember of the event itself. Luckily, I did not experience the memorial service, burial or other events which followed my death. I had never felt comfortable attending funerals and certainly had no desire to attend my own.

The actual day of my death started like most other days of my life. I woke up a little late that morning. Usually, I woke up at six-thirty. However on that day, I had overslept and it was dangerously close to seven. A very busy day lay ahead, starting with an eight o'clock meeting with my boss.

My boss had little tolerance for anyone being late, even if it was only by a few minutes. The man actually woke up around four in the morning. By seven-thirty in the morning, he had already spent an hour at the gym, commuted to the office from his home which was over an hour away, read his emails, reviewed his calendar, made his daily high protein smoothie shake and still apparently had plenty of time each morning to plan out new and exciting ways to create stress and irritation for me.

I gulped down two cups of coffee as I did each morning, took my shower, walked Barry, grabbed a granola bar and then prepared to jump in the car for the drive to work. On that morning, the coffee just would not seem to kick in and I still felt hopelessly groggy. I yearned for a return to my warm bed with Barry curled up at my feet.

I liked my coffee loaded with lots of cream and lots of sugar. Penny used to always say she liked her coffee like she liked her men, "strong and black." Although in reality, the only black man I knew she had ever dated would have qualified more appropriately as a "gentle cocoa." He was a sweetheart, but Penny's strong personality ended up being more than he could handle as was the case with so many of her potential suitors and ex-husbands. Penny used to joke that I liked my coffee like I liked my men, "rich and overly sweet." I often thought of this when I sipped my coffee and it always made me smile. It was probably true.

It was December 6, 2010 and Mother Nature had gifted us with another five inches or so of snow on top of the ten inches which had already covered the ground from previous snowfalls. The temperature was a pleasant and balmy twenty-three degrees above zero. The ground was extremely icy and so was my car. After carefully maneuvering my way through the icy parking lot, I spent an extra ten minutes clearing my car of snow and another ten minutes scraping ice off all the windows.

For those in warmer climates who are not accustomed to this joyous task, it only adds to the fun when you are still sleepy and running late. For some reason, I never seemed to have the foresight to start my car earlier and let the defroster do some of the work. That morning, I tried to convince myself that that all the scraping constituted a mini-workout since I would not be making it to the gym. Then again, who am I kidding, I hardly ever went to the gym. I still did, however, pay the monthly gym fee and proudly displayed my gym identification badge on my keychain, a testament to my healthy intentions.

In actuality, my biceps were a little sore after the intense scraping so maybe it would have qualified as a workout. By the time I was done with my scraping, I had become sufficiently cold and flustered. I cursed the Northeast and winter itself and warned no one in particular that I was seriously considering moving to a warmer climate.

Once the car was cleared off, I began my drive towards the office. On sunny days, my commute normally took only about fifteen minutes. However, when you add snow and ice into the mix, it could more than double the normal commute time. I fumbled with the radio trying to tune in something that sounded appealing and which might help provide me musical motivation.

I don't think I had a great singing voice, but I did love to sing. My car often served as my own little solitary mobile karaoke booth. I am not sure what others on the highway thought when I was fully enveloped in my solo musical performances. They probably thought my performances were loud and animated telephone conversations or, more likely than not, did not even notice me.

On that day, I remember that many stations were playing non-stop Christmas music. Although, I like a rousing Christmas carol as much as the next person, I was not awake enough or of a calm enough demeanor to deal with anything more profound than a rousing chorus of "Grandma Got Run Over By A Reindeer." I switched between channels but could only find droning NPR pledge drives which nauseated me a bit; corny DJs who apparently and erroneously thought they were hilarious which nauseated me more; and a conservative talk show bashing the President which just made me angry. I was not necessarily the biggest fan of the President, but he <u>was</u> now our President and I felt he was really doing his best to make positive changes in the country. I mean you have to give the guy a break. Would you want to be President? My job was just about all I could handle and I was really only responsible for myself. I couldn't even imagine being responsible for hundreds of millions of peoples' futures.

Since I had a busy and stressful day ahead of me, I thought maybe the soothing tunes of Mr. Barry Manilow might be just the ticket. Nothing soothed me more than Barry and me both singing a rousing rendition of "Mandy" or "I Write The Songs." Modern gal that I was, I had retired all of my old CDs and had imported them directly onto my smartphone.

Although I loved my SUV, it had not come equipped with Bluetooth and so I fumbled to connect the cable that linked my smartphone to my car stereo system. Although I managed to get the music started, somehow in my fumbling, the phone fell and wedged itself deep in the recesses separating the seat from the central cup holder console. It joined a colony of French Fries, drinking straw wrappers, discarded napkins, and various other remnants of on-the-go meals. I had every intention of giving my car a full vacuuming. This need was made even more urgent by the fact that I had given up fast food and had not visited a fast food establishment in at least three months. However, the corpses of past unhealthy meals remained lodged under the seat, joined now by my phone.

I continued to feel around for my missing phone. I clearly felt, at least this morning, that a morning without Barry was like a morning without sunshine. As I made my way onto the I-84 entrance ramp, I continued to sneak glances to see if I could spot the wayward phone. Although I swear I glanced down only for a millisecond, when I looked back to the road, I spotted another car less than thirty feet ahead of me at a dead stop. I slammed on my brakes and turned my steering wheel sharply to avoid a jarring collision.

I must have turned too sharply and slammed my brakes too hard because the last thing I remember was the car sliding to the left on a hidden patch of ice and slamming into the concrete barrier on the side of the entrance ramp. There was a loud crash and glass shattered everywhere. After that, for what seemed like a long time, the world went completely and utterly dark.

I don't remember any pain. All I really remember during that period of darkness was the haunting melody of "I Can't Smile Without You", softly playing in the background. It kind of pissed me off because I would have preferred to go out with a bouncier tune like "Copa Cabana. However, at least my death was accompanied by one of my favorite singers. At the very least, it may be one of the few deaths linked, at least indirectly to Barry Manilow.

Three

As the darkness enveloped me and the sound of Barry Manilow's voice faded into silence, I felt more completely alone but more completely relaxed than I ever had in my life. The feeling is hard to describe but it was somewhere between the sensation of being swaddled in a warm blanket and being suspended in a vat of warm mud. The darkness felt like it was enveloping me but also holding me in place.

I remained in this state for what seemed like a very long time. It could have been fifteen minutes or it could have been three months. It is difficult to estimate how much time has passed when you are immersed in total darkness. I began to realize how truly arbitrary our human notion of time is.

Eventually, the darkness began to disperse ever so slowly around me and the atmosphere started to take on a greenish glow. The green color is hard to describe, but it reminded me most of this white plastic bead necklace I had when I was a little girl. You would hold the beads up to the light and then shut yourself in the closet where they would glow a similarly eerie green color.

I fully expected the peaceful bright white light that so many people had described in their near-death experiences. I also anticipated long dead relatives materializing to welcome me to the afterlife. However, as is the case in life, assumptions are often the precursor to disappointment. I would have to settle for an eerie green glow and a warm respite from the chilly Northeast weather.

A while later, I had the strange feeling that my entire being was being sucked through a funnel. Not all feelings in the afterlife can be adequately described, but I went from feeling like I was taking up my normal size twelve amount of the atmosphere to being squeezed and compacted down into a small ball of energy. Although I was unable to see myself, I felt like I was probably about the size of a golf ball. I also felt totally energized like I just got out of an intense Zumba class and then immediately drank four energy drinks. I could almost feel electricity crackling off me. Truth be told, I had never attended a Zumba class but I did watch one on television once and I had truthfully consumed energy drinks on more than one occasion.

If this was Heaven, I thought it was a total rip-off. There were no streets paved in gold, no pearly gates and no angels singing heavenly music. There were no welcoming relatives, no white light and no personal meeting with Jesus. However, if this was Hell, this wasn't so bad. I could deal. I only knew a little about other religions but I was fairly certain this was not what the holy leaders of Buddhism, Islam and Hinduism predicted either. Well, I was nothing if not flexible in death. Of course, I mean flexible in a psychological way. As I mentioned, my gym habits left little to be desired, and I had reached an age where I was starting to pull muscles just by doing simple things like getting out of bed or turning around too quickly.

I was not able to really see my environment in the customary way but was able to sort of "feel" my environment in a way I had not experienced when I was alive. I could somehow feel colors, or lack thereof, and had a sense of the shape and size of objects around me. As I mentioned, there was no white light but the environment gave me more the sense of that weird twilight sort of lighting that you see just before full darkness sets in, albeit with a greenish tinge.

I then started to get the feeling of bouncing around rapidly like a racquet ball and a much wider assortment of colors filled my senses. Of course, I never played racquetball either because being shut up in one of those little rooms with that ball flying around at fifty miles an hour with some crazy competitive maniacal gym Nazi in spandex never seemed like fun to me. Like Zumba class, I had watched someone playing a few times though so I could definitely imagine what it was like. I still had no desire to actually play racquetball, but when you feel like the ball, well that my friend, is an entirely different and totally cool sensation.

After I somehow began to slow my ricocheting down to a less frenetic pace, I began to sense other little balls of energy around me moving around at various speeds. I could not see them but I could sense their energy fields as they passed. Some of them emanated a sense of peace and calmness, some emitted a sense of maniacal confusion and some had the distinct sense of anger and evil. The steady stream of energy continued to run through my new form. I still am not completely sure why I had not totally freaked out by this time, but I seemed to be getting used to the feeling of the energy running through me and it became familiar, comfortable and relatively peaceful.

Suddenly, I felt a tremendous jolt surge through me which felt foreign, unnatural and unwelcomed. I sensed what I believed to be a male voice say to me angrily. "What the fuck? Watch where you're going!" and then zip away. Here I was, dead, and apparently there were even assholes in the afterlife. Shortly after that, I felt another energy surge... this one, a lot more soothing but also stimulating, like peppermint tea. And yes, I have consumed peppermint tea! A different male voice said "Hello. You must be new here. The name is Stuart."

"My name is Della," I replied, "And I have no idea where I am or what is happening."

"Understandable." Stuart replied, "Follow me and we can get to a calmer place and we'll compare notes. I can tell you have a good energy and I'd definitely like to get to know you better." Here I was dead, and apparently getting hit on by another energy ball.

"Sure," I replied and followed him. I mean why not? I had all the time in the world.

Without really knowing how or why, I followed him in a whizzing erratic path to a place that seemed to have less chaos and which felt a little more peaceful. In life, I would never have indiscriminately followed a strange man, but I was fairly certain violent crime was not much of an issue in energy ball world. In addition, as previously mentioned, complimenting me was a sure way to persuade me to do anything. Pathetic? Perhaps. But let's not be judgy!

Four

I must say Stuart was polite, funny and quite engaging. Where were the nice guys like this when I was alive? We chatted and discussed the situation where we had both found ourselves. Stuart had been in this realm for quite a while. However, when there is no real sense of time or space, it is hard to quantify what "a while" is.

He had succumbed to cancer at the age of thirty-six and left his wife and two young children aged eight and six behind. He missed his children terribly but his relationship with his wife had been tenuous at best right up until the end. The only reason they conceived children at all, according to Stuart, was due to his wife Lisa's love of Cosmopolitans and the temporary memory lapses they produced, causing her to forget how much she disliked him.

She was nicer to him in his final days though, he recalled, causing him to wonder if she had stopped by a nearby cocktail lounge for Happy Hour before heading to the hospice center for her final goodbyes. She had held his hand, assured him she and the children would be fine, encouraged him to head towards the light and continually pressed him for more specifics of his life insurance policy and any other money he may have "squirreled away." He did miss her in his own way, he admitted, and he hoped he could find some way to channel his energy, manifest himself somehow again in the human realm and scare the shit out of her one dark night.

Stuart had been a quasi-practicing Roman Catholic and indicated he was a little disappointed with the afterlife thus far. He had expected to meet God, Jesus or at least have one of the saints do a meet and greet. Instead, like me, he had found himself deposited in this foreign place with few answers and an endless list of questions.

He did indicate his happiness at not being ushered into the burning pits of Hell for a few questionable business deals, using the Lord's name in vain an infinite number of times, occasionally fantasizing about killing his wife and perhaps spending a few too many hours perusing Asian porn sites. He still held out hope of seeing Heaven and believed himself to be in some sort of purgatory state where his soul was being cleansed although Stuart admitted, "that could take one hell of a long time."

Stuart had encountered many energy balls, souls, spirits or whatever we actually were. Many were new to the realm and had recently experienced death although quite a few had been around for a while like Stuart. Each had their own perspective on what was happening.

Some, like Stuart, thought they must be in a temporary place awaiting a welcome into Heaven or a final spiritual kingdom. Perhaps, Heaven was too full and we were all waiting for a spot to open up, like a sought-after apartment in a very desirable apartment building. Others felt they would be reincarnated into another human existence and were awaiting dispatch into a new body. Still, others suspected that they were trapped in a spirit realm in which they needed to take care of unresolved business before they could move on. In addition, there was the contingent of which I was a part. This group had no idea what was going on and were just waiting for something to happen that would shed some much needed light on this situation.

Stuart and I found creative ways to pass the time together. It was nice spending time with a man, or at least a masculine energy, where neither of us did, or even could, fixate on the physical aspects of each other. Our connection was, at least initially, exclusively non-physical. It was a nice change. One of our favorite discussions was coming up with Top Ten Lists of why it was not so bad to be dead. His favorite was not having to go to the bathroom and the associated afflictions of diarrhea, constipation and painful gaseous bloating. I personally liked not having to shave my legs, worry about whether the grays were showing through since my last coloring, and filing my taxes.

We also came up with stupid jokes about our condition that would make us laugh uncontrollably. For example, why did the energy ball refuse a glass of milk at breakfast? Because she was already all juiced up. OK. Maybe you don't think that one is so funny, but believe me it was a big hit in the afterlife.

We eventually found we could rub up against each other and kind of pool our energies. It gave me this intense, glorious and indescribable feeling. It actually reminded me of an extended orgasm, making my energy rise to a new level and my whole existence seeming to be more powerful, electric and spectacular. It was during one of these sessions of innocent energy ball heavy petting that something unbelievable happened, which brings me to the next chapter in this crazy story!

Five

I always wondered how there could be enough room in Heaven for everyone with so many dead people already there and with new recruits showing up every minute. I mean people have been dying for hundreds of thousands of years. Wouldn't there be an overabundance of souls in Heaven? Although this spiritual realm or energy ball commune was majorly busy and at times felt like the interstate with entities whizzing by, it certainly would be even busier if everyone from Agnes the cavewoman to me were jetting around for eternity. Of course, I had no idea if there were other realms or what the deal really was.

I did know there was me, Della, the energy ball, heretofore known as the *rubber*... and Stuart, the energy ball, heretofore known as the *rubbee*. Both *rubber* and *rubbee* were having a glorious time as previously described, smashing into each other and enjoying the energy rush.

In retrospect, we may have gotten a little too aggressive. What started out as a brief and gentle bumping which brought us small pleasures, had become a little addictive. Before I knew what was happening, we were charging at each other like a toreador and a bull at an extremely passionate bullfight. On one of our passionate ball bounces, I heard a "pop" and then Stuart was gone. What had previously been a momentary surge of energy for me became a constant surge of energy. Where I had felt a constant buzz of energy before, I now felt a consistently powerful "throb" of energy. I felt as if I was now somehow bigger and more powerful.

Although I don't want to say I killed Stuart, I believed I had usurped his energy and integrated it with my own. I felt sad that my friend was now gone but at least he had gone out on a pleasurable rush. I felt a bit like the female grasshopper who bit the head off the male after mating. I still don't know what happened to Stuart's spirit, but I like to think he lives on in my energy makeup.

What was truly strange is that since I had no idea of Stuart's actual physical appearance, I could not visually see him in my mind's eye. My memory was solely of his essence and the positive feeling I had in his company. I liked to think I now had a bit of masculine energy in me as well and perhaps that would make me a more well-rounded being. I mean if you are going to be an energy ball, it is probably good to be "well-rounded." Apparently, I was becoming an energy ball comedian as well. Keep reading folks, I've got a million of them!

After that experience, I pledged to hold off on bumping up against any other balls for the time being or at least until I got a better handle on how things worked in this environment. After all, I did not want to get a reputation as an afterlife "man-eater" and did not want to lose another friend due to what was apparently my unbridled energy ball passion. I buzzed around for quite a while trying to figure out what to do next. Pulsating with my newly expanded power, I must admit that I did find myself just waiting for another energy ball to give me any crap. I was on top of the world and felt like Queen Energy Ball, ready to take on the world. Penny would be proud.

I floated around for a while longer to try and get a sense of my surroundings. It is difficult to explain how things appeared in that afterlife energy world. Although I could not visually "see" in the classic sense, I definitely could sense the other energy balls around me. I somehow knew their size, color and general demeanor. The environment we were in was fairly bland although different areas did seem to emanate different colors and different emotions. This new world was devoid of physical objects in the normal sense and therefore seemed infinite and without borders of any sort. I spent my time buzzing around at various speeds orienting myself as best I could. It was strange, new and wonderful in a way, but was also lonely, especially with Stuart no longer there to welcome and comfort me.

With my newfound energy, I started experiencing something else new as well. I began to hear voices. They were faint and melded into the background but they were definitely voices. At first, I could not really understand them. It sounded a bit like the whining of a fan or a radio station that was not completely tuned in. Once I focused, the voices started to become clearer.

There were multiple voices so it was very difficult to figure out what was being said, but there was one word I heard clearly time and time again. It was a distinct and powerful word and was, if truth be told, one of my favorites. "Della!" Now I don't know about you but I could be ignoring an entire conversation and as soon as my name is spoken, my ears prick up.

As I listened more closely, I heard a familiar voice speaking amidst the cacophony, "Della if you are out there, please show us a sign of your presence. Della, we miss you. Della, are you there? Della, we are here at your home in hopes of reaching you." Who was it? The voice sounded so familiar. Then it hit me. It was my brother's wife Janet. Memories of how uncomfortable she made me filled my thoughts. In addition, memories of how much I loved the bargain skirt I purchased on my last visit to see her and my brother also permeated my brain. Although I generally hated shopping, I certainly did love that Danny's Discount Dress Barn.

As I listened more intently to the voices while trying to suppress my less than positive memories of Janet, I heard another voice, more faint but still audible. It was saying. "She is with us. I can feel her energy now. I am seeing… this is strange… but is there some connection to a place called Danny's?" Then I heard my sister-in-law's perfect voice saying. "Oh my God, that is her. She LOVED Danny's Discount. I mean I am not sure WHY she loved Danny's, but she certainly loved those bargains."

Terrific, my first connection back to the world of the living and it comes in the form of Danny's Discount Dress Barn. Even in death, I felt inferior. I tried my best to focus on something more appropriate but no matter what I did, I now could not get Danny's Discount Dress Barn out of my brain.

I must admit I loved the plum skirt I bought on that last trip to Rhode Island and Danny's definitely did seem to have some of the best prices on bras in New England. They should have really opened one up in Connecticut, although I happily drove to Rhode Island to shop there. In fact, I had a large number of shopping trips where I did not even drive the extra fifteen minutes to see my brother and Janet. I was fairly certain I would not run into Janet or my brother at Danny's or at Julio's, the greasy diner in Providence where I loved to grab lunch during these shopping trips.

The second voice turned out to be a medium Janet had consulted with. I did not learn until later, her actual name was Elizabeth so I have referred to her by the nickname I gave her, Psychic Suzie, throughout most of the rest of my story. I have also since learned there is a difference between a psychic and a medium, but "psychic" sounds so much more intriguing than "medium."

"There is definitely a strong connection to a place called Danny's. It is coming through loud and clear," Psychic Suzie confirmed.

"Wow. I wonder why she is fixated on Danny's?" Janet pondered. "We did go shopping there. Well, she went shopping there the last time she visited us. I wasn't feeling well and waited in the car. Maybe, there's a lack of shopping in Heaven? I mean, I wouldn't think that you would need to worry about buying four dollar dresses in Heaven. That is a little strange. I would think she would not have to worry about what she is wearing at all. I mean she was always dressed in a more 'casual' style anyway. Do spirits even wear clothes? Are they naked? Oh, I certainly hope Della's not naked…"

"She is probably just remembering your last interaction," Suzie interrupted. "And I am pretty sure she is not in Heaven at the moment, I believe she is in some transitional state."

Janet was a real piece of work. For the record, it was not a four dollar dress, it was a ten dollar skirt. Well, truth be told, I probably would have bought a four dollar dress if I found one but that wasn't the point. I mean Danny's was full of bargains but they weren't giving things away. One had to be careful though. Once I had bought a beautiful green swimsuit at Danny's in anticipation of an upcoming trip to Mexico. However, the dye had run out and tinged my buttocks and chest a crazy shade of green. It took almost a week to fade. Luckily, no one had the privilege of seeing me in the nude during my "green" period and believe me, it was a sight!

"Oh my," Psychic Suzie began, "I am now seeing… well I am seeing… um… never mind… it's not important.

"Right on, Suzie," I thought. "No need to bring that up!" I was pretty sure that vision would stick in her head for some time to come.

Six

As I listened to Janet and her psychic guide continue to try to communicate with me, I started thinking more about my human existence. Memories of my mother, my brother, my dog Barry and my best friend Penny flooded my thoughts. As the memories flashed by, Suzie picked up on them and duly reported them back to Janet. It was incredible but I also must say that Psychic Suzie totally made up some stuff I didn't say, think or have any connection to.

At one point, I heard Psychic Suzie say "Della wants you to know you were a very important part of her life. She sends her love and wants you to know she is at peace." I can assure you that message never crossed my mind! I did not send love and I was not at peace. Unbelievable, but I guess mediums may grant themselves some creative license in this area.

As my memories continued to flash before me, I remembered something that had weighed on my mind for years that I wished I had resolved before kicking the bucket. This may sound stupid and inconsequential to you and may be reflective of how terribly unexciting some may think my life was, but it was something that still haunted my memories so many years later. The psychic-infused trip down memory lane only served to bring it to the forefront and I began to feel like I should not move on without resolving it somehow.

It was a story I had kept to myself for many years. The only person I had ever revealed it to was Penny during a particularly revealing game of Truth or Dare. I am not sure if we were the only grown women who still played Truth or Dare, but that is how I roll.

Although it had continued to haunt me for all these years, it was nothing compared to some of the "truths" Penny revealed about herself. Let's just say that Penny had quite the colorful past and could have quite the colorful temper. She had enacted a series of retributory actions against former boyfriends and husbands as well as a couple of female friends who had double-crossed her. Some of these actions could have resulted in imprisonment for grand larceny, assault and breaking and entering. Unlike me, she was not very repentant. Although she was not caught, she still felt like the punishments she inflicted on her adversaries were not only appropriate but perhaps not harsh enough.

Although she had mellowed somewhat with age, I can confirm it was still not a good idea to cross Penny.

Now, back to my little act of sin. When I was twenty-two years old and a waitress at an Irish pub in Boston called McAllister's, before I started my exciting life in the insurance world, and when I was still finishing up some classes at the Boston College, I had done what was perhaps one of the most regrettable things in my life. It was something that still made me feel like a jerk and something completely out of character for me. I still am not sure why I did it or why I carried that baggage along with me all these years, but Janet's and Psychic Suzie's connection with me brought it front and center.

Back then, as we did each night when we closed the restaurant, a bunch of us girls would take over one of the booths, grab a drink and add up our tips for the evening. This particular night had not been a good night for me. It was a slow night to begin with, and there had been a bunch of senior citizens who took up one of my prime tables for hours and left me a meager tip. In addition, another table had never-ending issues with their meals and had created such a continual fuss that our manager, Matt, finally just comped their whole meal just to get them out of the restaurant. No tip was included which also caused my income that night to be unusually unprofitable. My lack of money was causing me a little extra stress because my rent was due and I had recently spent what little savings I had to fix my piece of junk car.

After sucking down a more powerful than needed Rum and Coke, heavy on the rum light on the Coke, I decided to take a break from the exciting exercise of counting my non-existent tips and excused myself to visit the ladies room. While finishing up a satisfying pee and wondering how wrong and/or pathetic it would be for me to stuff a bunch of the wax paper-like sheets that served as toilet paper into my purse for home use, I spotted a pink cashmere sweater hanging merrily on the back of the stall door.

I was amazed I had missed it before as its cheery pink aura contrasted significantly with the sad nondescript beige of the stall door. After dabbing myself dry, I unhooked the sweater from the door with every intention of adding it to our bin of unclaimed goods at the front of the restaurant. As I examined the sweater in further detail, I found something in a cute little hidden pocket inside the sweater. It was a roll of bills. The roll consisted of two hundred twenty-five dollars, which was, by my estimation, a small fortune in those days.

Before I knew what was happening, I had slipped the money in my pocket, returned the sweater to its hook, and left the restaurant with the newfound cash. It was the wrong thing to do. However, desperate times call for desperate measures I told myself, and these were desperate times for me.

I wrote a number of stories in my head trying to ease my guilt. Perhaps, the owner of the cashmere was a drug dealer. I mean there were lots of pink cashmere-wearing female drug dealers in Boston, right? Perhaps, she was just a rich spoiled bitch who had more money than she needed. I mean it was cashmere and who walks around with two hundred twenty-five dollars hidden in a cashmere sweater? I also surmised that like most of the items that languished in our Lost and Found bin, it would probably go unclaimed. So many drunk college girls wandered in and out of McAllister's with it being just one of many stops along their tour of intoxication, they probably would not even remember where they left it.

I told myself that it was a reward from above. I was meant to find it. It was placed there for me to find. It was the answer to my current debt-ridden crisis. As soon as I got home, I put two hundred dollars of my findings into an envelope, knocked on my landlord's door, presented him with the dirty money and consoled myself with the fact that I could live in my rattrap apartment another month.

Everything may have been fine if I had not come into work the next day to find one of my fellow waitresses, Cindy Benson, crying and expressing disbelief at the fact that someone could be so low to take the money she planned to use for rent that month from her sweater that she had inadvertently left in the bathroom. "Who would be such a jerk?" she pondered loudly in between gasps and sobs. I told her it would have to be a real big asshole.

Our manager Matt took up a collection and all the girls contributed what they could. I made a comparatively substantial contribution of twenty-five dollars. "You are such an angel Della!" Cindy said with tears in her eyes. "The world would be such a better place if there were more people in it like you."

"It's the least I can do for a friend," I told her, as my guilt increased tenfold. I regretted saying that to this day.

The one big time crappy thing I did and I still carried the guilt more than twenty years later. Why I never fessed up, I will never know. I mean it wasn't like I took it out of her purse, but still it seemed dishonest and even more damning because I never admitted to it after the fact.

"Does the name Cindy Bronson… err, Benson… yes definitely Cindy Benson… does that name mean anything to you?" Psychic Suzie suddenly asked Janet.

"There is some unresolved issue involving money with someone by that name", she said matter-of-factly. What the hell? I thought I told the psychic what to say. How did she get into my head? "Don't say that!" I pleaded. "Don't say that!" I yelled.

"No. I am not aware of anyone with that name, although it does seem like a pretty common name," Janet answered.

"I believe Della is telling me she worked with her when she was younger, maybe as a waitress or something like that.... perhaps in a bar... yes... it feels like it was in a bar... and it feels like she can't move on until she receives forgiveness from this woman. She wronged her in some way. I am not sure what it was, but it was something involving money. It is definitely something involving money that is causing her not to be able to move on."

"I can move on," I pleaded. "I can move on! Don't tell Goodie-Two-Shoes Janet that!" However, I had to admit, this psychic lady was pretty good.

Psychic Suzie then ad-libbed, "and Della tells me you're the one who can help her! She is saying you're the one who can help her make this situation right."

Okay… now Suzie was just making stuff up again. I may have carried some guilt but I certainly didn't want Janet to help with anything.

I then heard Janet's voice say. "I will make this right. I will find this Cindy Benson. I do know Della worked in a tavern called McAllister's when she was in school. My husband and I used to go visit her there when we were dating. Come to think of it, I actually do remember a Cindy and her last name may very well have been Benson. That sounds right. She was one of the waitresses who worked there with Della. My husband will definitely know because he spent a lot of time there with Della. I believe that bar, McAllister's I think it was called, is actually still in operation. At least it was a year or so ago when we last were in Boston. We stopped there for a bit of nostalgia. I bet we will be able to locate her. I'll also get the family together to say goodbye to Della. I want Della to be free and I know the rest of her family and friends would want the same. Thank you so much for your help. You are amazing!"

I certainly hoped the charge for the psychic channeling was less than the two hundred twenty five dollars I had absconded with but then again Janet was not into bargains.

Seven

The session with Psychic Suzie had apparently ended or maybe I had just lost my connection. I strained to hear something else but all I could hear was silence. The silence was suddenly replaced by lots of voices, almost like I switched a channel on the radio. I tried to return my consciousness to the energy ball universe. The voices were making me a little nauseous and I also was now feeling increasingly tired and drained. You may wonder how an energy ball can feel nauseous. I can't answer that question. For all I knew, I could have been pregnant after the interlude with Stuart and a baby energy ball could have been forthcoming.

One voice was saying "Tell Isabell that I love her." Another jockeying to be heard above the clatter yelled "I am OK. Let them know I am OK." And then the voice of what sounded like an elderly Southern woman repeated incessantly "I am innocent. I didn't kill him! I didn't kill him!" It took me a bit to realize these voice were not coming from Psychic Suzie's den of spiritualist phenomena but were emanating from a crowd of energy balls who had now gathered all about me.

The elderly voice cried out even stronger. "Come on y'all, tell them I didn't do it! Tell them Minerva Jackson did not kill her husband. Tell them Minerva is innocent!" I sensed the Minerva Jackson voice was coming from an energy ball that was very close to me and throbbing an angry red. The voice continued in a hostile, but somehow still grandmotherly Southern tone. "Goddamn it. Y'all blew it. You had a damn connection and you blew it! I had a chance to clear my name and now who knows when I'll get that chance again!"

Now I am usually a pretty amiable person but I felt like I was being assaulted by this aggressive Southern grandma. "Listen Minerva... or whatever your name is... leave me alone! This is all new to me and I don't know what I am doing. I'm sorry that I couldn't let them know that you were innocent but you'll have to make your own psychic connection and stop hassling me." I am not sure if my newfound assertiveness was the result of the energy I had acquired from Stuart or if I just was reaching my breaking point with my world having been turned upside down.

47

"I'm so sorry baby. I just got excited and carried away. It's so rare for someone to be able to communicate with the living folks," she apologized.

"It's OK," I said. "I can imagine it must be difficult to have died without clearing your name. It must really be horrible to have people think you did something horrific that you didn't."

"Ooooh baby," the voice responded. "Bless your heart. I killed the bastard. I stabbed him with a screwdriver. Right up through the ribs! I should have gutted him like a deer. And baby, he wasn't the only one! I just don't want them to think I did it." This was then punctuated by a long series of Southern cackles. "I'd do it again. I'd do it again and again. Kill the bastards! Kill the bastards!" Minerva's voice seemed to somehow punctuate the air again with its incessant cackling. The cackling was very creepy. It made me feel like I had connected with Dolly Parton's crazy homicidal older sister.

Meanwhile, I was surrounded by what appeared to be dozens of other energy balls, all clamoring for my attention and asking me to communicate messages for them. I pushed my way through the crowd of buzzing balls as they bumped up next to me pleading, crying and clamoring. I felt like my glorious Barry Manilow, navigating through a group of overexcited fans.

One of the balls, with a stronger energy than the others and glowing a curious pink color uttered in a conspiratorial tone with a strong New York accent "Hey honey. You're one of us now. That crazy lady Minerva is right. You have the gift to connect. It is rare. We need to stick together though. My name is Daphne. Pleased to make your acquaintance."

"I'm Della." I said, "Great to meet you too. But who are you referring to? Who is us?"

The voice chuckled and said. "Well, we call ourselves the Pink Ladies. You know like in Grease? We'd love to have you join us. We all have the ability to connect with the living. It is like a club for those of us with the gift. When you have the ability to connect with the living, you can get pretty much anything you want around here."

"Really?" I laughed. "Like what a new pair of shoes? And what about the men? What about the children? Don't they have the ability too? I imagine they're not part of the Pink Ladies."

"Of course some men have the ability. " she laughed "But there are definitely way more women than men with the gift. Besides, most of the men with the gift I have encountered would rather be left to themselves and frankly, that is just fine with us ladies too. Well, we did let Martin in because he makes us laugh and he doesn't mind being called a Pink Lady. As far as children, I really don't know. There are only a handful of children's spirits I have encountered in this realm and I am not aware of any who have the gift."

"Girlfriend…" a man's voice said from behind me. "I don't mind being called a Pink Lady, but I have most certainly not sworn off men. Even in my current state, I find them enthralling. Della, I just know we are going to be the best of friends. You are going to be a princess in this realm. I can tell. But just remember, there is only room for one queen. Do you feel me?"

"Della… you'll get used to Martin," Daphne assured me. "He just likes to have fun, but sometimes, he is just over the top. Come this way and we'll introduce you to the rest of the girls. I think you're going to fit in here just fine. The way you responded to Minerva shows you got chutzpah, which is exactly what you need to survive around here!"

I made my way through the crowd of energy balls and followed my new friends. She was right. I really felt I was going to fit in and that was not a feeling I was altogether used to.

Eight

I spent a lot of time with Martin and Daphne, along with a group of other "Pink Lady" energy balls and enjoyed myself immensely. I must say it is quite interesting when you get to know someone without knowing what they look like physically. I hoped that I had not been too shallow of a person in life. However, I certainly cannot say truthfully that my personal assessment of many people was not, at least initially, at least partially, based on their physical appearance, especially when they are nude and playing Frisbee.

For all I know in life, Daphne could have been a gorgeous six foot New York City glamazon whose beauty may have intimidated me from ever getting to know her. She could have also been a morbidly obese woman whose face was covered with warts and lesions. The point is, here in the afterlife, it really didn't matter. The only beauty that mattered was the beauty of an individual's spirit and both Daphne and Martin, had humorous and fun spirits and I was so happy to have come into contact with them.

Daphne, as it turned out had actually been from Paramus, New Jersey and had died fairly young at the age of twenty-six in a skiing accident while on vacation in Colorado with her husband of two years. Her husband had looked on in horror as she accidentally took a wrong turn off a marked trail and skied tragically off a cliff. She had held on for days in the hospital with a broken neck, broken back, punctured lung and other internal injuries before slowly passing from the world of the living with her husband at her side. The pain she felt in that hospital bed, she said, was nothing like the pain she felt with losing the love of her life.

She had been able to make psychic connections with her husband on a number of occasions but finally had decided, that after assuring him she was alright, it was too emotionally draining for both her and him to continue the communication. The greatest gift she could give him was to let him move on as she somewhat hesitatingly had done. She had apparently been in this realm for at least twenty human years since she indicated she had died in 1989. She was the de facto leader of the "Pink Ladies", although Martin may have argued otherwise.

Martin was a fun and energetic fellow who did exhibit the stereotypical characteristics of a flamboyant gay man, although at times, I could not help but feel that some of it was put on for the entertainment of the rest of us. Whatever the case, he was a strong, vibrant and fun spirit who filled our afterlives with endless laughter.

In reality, I had known a significant number of gay men over the years. Only a handful of them were even remotely as colorful as Martin. Most of the gay men I had known were almost boringly average. Although I'm not sure any of them could be classified as "super-masculine", few of them would have stood out in a crowd of straight men either.

Martin had died in 1995 at the age of fifty-two from what he believed must have been a stroke, heart attack or possibly an aneurysm. He had been with his partner for nine years at the time and they lived in the Hampden section of Baltimore, Maryland. Martin had gone to bed feeling a little under the weather and with what he thought was a bad case of indigestion. He awoke suddenly in the night with a pain surging through his entire body. He said everything went bright white for a moment and then everything went dark. He was then on his way to departing the human realm. His partner Jose had slept through the whole thing.

Martin had not been able to connect with Jose despite several attempts which saddened him. "One has to be open to the possibility of speaking to the dead," Martin explained. Jose thought the whole realm of psychics, ghosts, and for that matter any kind of afterlife, was preposterous and the product of peoples' overactive imaginations and need for control.

"Grrrl, "Martin quipped, "I only hope the best for him. I miss him, but hope he has found someone to love. Of course, I can't expect he would find anyone nearly as fabulous as me! If he does, they had better treat him well," warned Martin. "If anyone ever hurts my Jose, I will find out about it somehow and claw the bastard's eyes out. I don't know how I will do it but I will find a way." I didn't doubt him.

The other "Pink Ladies" were a motley assortment of personalities, each with their own stories and histories which made for interesting conversations.

There was Gloria, a retired Real Estate Agent from Colorado Springs who had succumbed to breast cancer in her late sixties. "The only positive thing about that awful cancer..." she recalled, "...was that for the first time in my life, just before my death, I probably could have fit into a size two."

There was Marina from Chihuahua, Mexico who had worked in a textile factory most of her life. It was a job she detested. Although she did miss her family, the taste of food and the beauty of Mexico, she admitted she definitely did not miss getting up early every day to go to her job. Marina had died in 2009 in a fire at her factory building at the age of thirty-nine.

Kelly Sue from Nashville, Tennessee was another vibrant personality with her mix of sweet Southern belle charm and no-nonsense organized approach to life and death. Kelly Sue had apparently inherited a lot of money from her deceased husband whose real name I never learned as she always referred to him as Butter Bean. When I asked her about what career she had been involved in prior to her death. She responded, "Career? Oh no… no… no! Butter Bean would never allow me to work! If I had pursued a career, I am just sure he would have rolled over in his grave. My little Butter Bean made sure I was well taken care of before and after his untimely demise. I do miss my little Butter Bean and I know I will see him before too much more time passes."

Kelly Sue had apparently died at age sixty-three from kidney failure after a particularly bad infection had mysteriously and quickly attacked her kidneys and other organs. When she suspected her life was very close to coming to an end, she had insisted that someone come to the hospital to do her hair, fix her makeup and assist her in writing up individualized farewell cards to all of her friends and family. "Dying," she explained in her delicate Southern drawl, "...is not an excuse for bad manners."

Others in the "Pink Lady" family included Renee, a bank clerk from Nice, France; Debbie, a seventeen year old fast food worker from Decatur, Kentucky; Marlene, a forty-seven year old truck driver from Ottawa, Canada; Meriem, a twenty-four year old mother of two from Algeria; and Bo Mi, a thirty-five year old homemaker from rural China. There were others but these were the ones whom I remember best.

Although I felt like everyone was speaking to me in English, or at least that is how I heard it in my head, apparently, language was somewhat irrelevant in the afterlife. We were all able to communicate in what appeared to be a universal language. All the Pink Ladies taught me lessons about communicating with the living. Some of the lessons I learned from them included the following:

1. It is not possible to communicate with anyone from the human realm who is not interested in communicating with you.

2. Communicating with the human realm takes up a lot of energy and you must be careful not to exhaust yourself.

3. If you have enough energy, you can sometimes manifest yourself, move items or create sounds but only for very brief periods.

4. You periodically will want to replenish your energy by connecting with and obtaining energy from another energy ball or you may lose your ability to communicate. In addition, your energy will increase on its own over time albeit at a slower rate.

5. If you use too much energy, your energy disappears and no one really knows what happens to you when that occurs. There were a fair number of "missing in action" energy balls who had apparently depleted their reserves and disappeared in a "pop" of energy. This included some former Pink Ladies who were never heard from again.

6. Communication with the human realm took practice and you needed to "tune-in" to hear those who were attempting to communicate.

7. Other spirits or "energy balls" in this realm are so desperate to make contact with the human realm that they will do anything for you if you assist them.

In addition to these unwritten rules which most of the group agreed were true, most also agreed that there was no shortage of surprises and still a lot of unknowns. No one was still really sure completely what might happen to them in their present or future state. "The only thing we are all certain of," said Martin, "is that we're not certain of shit." I couldn't have agreed with him more.

Nine

I spent lots of time with the "Pink Ladies" practicing my ability to communicate. They taught me how to "tune in" better to the messages from the human world. "Tuning In" was a bit like meditation which I remembered from my Buddhist phase. My Buddhist phase had been one of many phases I had gone through in my lifetime including my organic food only phase, my "I'm going to cut out wheat and sugar" phase, my juicing phase, my bicycling phase, my knitting phase, my protein shake phase, my "I'm going to stop shaving my legs" phase, my "I'm going to the gym every day because it's not a diet, it's a lifestyle" phase and the "I am so sick of worrying about what people think of me, I am going to get fat, drink margaritas on weeknights, eat ice cream, watch TV for three straight days if I want and everyone can kiss my ass phase." OK... I hadn't actually started that last phase yet but I had planned on doing so before I died.

At any rate, "tuning in" was pretty awesome and at the beginning perhaps just a bit frightening. You found the quietest place you could away from the buzzing energy ball freeway, tried to silence your mind of all other thoughts and just listened to the silence. At first, nothing much happened for me, but then slowly, I began to hear voices just as I had heard when Psychic Suzie attempted to contact me. They started out as a low hum like the motor of a fan when the rest of the house is silent. Then, they sounded like whispers, barely audible. Gradually, I heard lots of voices. All of these voices were seemingly talking over one another like the murmur of a crowd in a busy train station. Daphne urged me to choose one of the voices and focus on it, blocking out the rest and attempting to communicate solely with it.

I initially expected that the only voices I would hear would be from psychics and those allegedly skilled in communication with the afterlife. My expectation was also that I would only hear voices with messages intended for me. However, the truth was there were infinite voices. All trying to connect in different ways with someone who had passed.

I tried to focus on one voice. It was a sweet little voice almost drowned out by all the others. "Mama," it said. "Mama. I hope you can hear me. I miss you so much. I am doing my best to be a good girl. If you are out there, please send me a sign. It is so hard without you here. I hope you are in Heaven with all the other angels. I miss you so much."

My entire being swelled with sadness and pity. I am not sure energy balls can cry but I had that feeling you get when emotion swells in your chest. "Oh you poor little baby." I thought. "I am sure your Mama is fine and loves and misses you very much. "

"Is that you?" the little girl's voice responded. I could tell her voice was filled with love and hope. "Mama... I can hear you. I can hear you a little. Mama?"

"Your mama is fine sweetheart and she sends her love." I repeated over and over. "Your mama loves you very much and misses you too. She wants you to be a good girl"

There was silence for a bit and then I heard the little girl voice say "I can hear you Mama. I love you Mama. I am so glad you are all right."

Oh no. This little girl thought I was her mother. What was I doing? Maybe her mother was not all right at all. Had I been deceptive? At the very least, the little girl seemed more at peace and thankful.

Daphne explained that the communication with the human realm was not always so crystal clear. Sometimes people only received the "feelings" and not necessarily the words, especially if the recipient was not a skilled medium. She assured me that my communication of love and assurance was what the little girl needed and that I had served my purpose. She also urged me to take a rest before I exhausted too much energy.

I continued to practice my communication and although I got very good at focusing in on people's voices, I became increasingly hesitant to communicate back with people who had specific requests. I mean how was I going to help Harold find his wife Patricia? It is not like I could put a sign in this afterlife world that read *WANTED: A woman named Patricia who had a husband Harold, please email me at Della@energyball.com for more information.*

I did have some fun with people who were communicating along the lines of "Is anyone out there?" I had entertaining conversations with psychics practicing their communication skills as well as teenagers attempting to contact the dead. I may have embellished some aspects of my life. I must also admit that I may have just completely made up stories pretending to be Bette Davis, Jack the Ripper, Janis Joplin, a woman from the Salem Witch Trials and Courtney Love. The last one didn't work out so well since apparently Courtney Love is still alive. Oh well, a girl has to have some fun even in the afterlife and I must admit it was a little fun freaking out the teenagers. Just remember, if you receive communication from the beyond, dead people can bullshit you as much as the next person. I just hope Janis Joplin's energy ball doesn't show up around here soon. I am fairly certain that she could kick my energy ball butt.

I also started taking requests from other energy balls. They would give me the names of friends and relatives they wished to communicate with and I would send out a signal reciting the name over and over and listening for a voice to respond. In most cases, this didn't work but in some cases, it did. When it did, it was totally draining but very satisfying for all parties involved. I learned how to receive transferred energy from other balls to pump up my reserves. I also learned that, as had been the case with Stuart, if I was too aggressive or excited during this transfer, I could completely suck the energy out of the other entity and "pop" they would be gone.

I must say that the fact that I apparently drained some energy balls dry and made them disappear did not diminish the desire of other energy balls to continue to submit their requests to me. Other than increasing my energy significantly, I did not feel any different when this occurred. I retained my personality and did not appear to integrate any of their personalities into my own. Certainly, this did not happen often and I did my best to try and disassociate myself during energy transfers if the transfer session started to become uncontrollable.

In one circumstance, during one of my very low energy days, I encountered an energy ball, who in exchange for my attempt to contact one of her children, almost drained my energy. It was the one and only time this occurred to me and luckily I was able to disengage before my energy was completely depleted. The feeling was significantly different than normal. Rather than my energy increasing during the transfer session, I felt it growing weaker and weaker. It took me quite a while to recover after that session. That energy ball had a unique "fuzzy" feeling about it when I came close to it. From that point forward, I declined any requests from energy balls who gave me a similar feeling. In addition, I never allowed my energy to dip that low again.

Ten

It was also around this time that despite my newfound celebrity, I discovered not everyone was a fan. I mean what was I doing wrong? I was helping people make contact with the human realm. It was like reverse channeling. I was becoming the afterlife version of the Long Island Medium and who doesn't like the Long Island Medium? I just needed a contract and maybe I could have my own show on TLC! However, apparently not all energy balls were cut from the same proton pool because the Pink Ladies had a detractor who most assuredly did not approve of what they were doing.

In the midst of one our collective psychic sessions as I was merrily providing details of my life to an energetic psychic named Bruno, I felt an energy ball collide into me with gentle but persistent force. The energy ball, which I had never seen before and which was glowing a unique blue color, was shouting at me in a persistent and powerful male voice, "Stop It! Stop It! Stop the evil! Repent! This is not the path of the righteous! Stop this and join us sister in our quest for salvation and forgiveness. Leave this den of sinners if you wish to see the beauty of Heaven. Join us or you will be forced to remain in this state of purgatory forever."

I then heard Martin's voice say "Jackson. If you don't leave her alone, I will suck the energy right out of you right now. And baby, ask anyone… I can suuuuuccck!"

The male voice responded, "Martin. There is no need to be vulgar. I am trying to save this soul before you and your band of sinful thieves can corrupt her soul any further. It is her choice whether she wants to be saved, not yours. Gentle soul, do you wish to join us and point yourself towards the light and away from the darkness? Point yourself towards salvation and not damnation?"

Martin's voice responded. "Jackson… baby. Her name is Della not 'gentle soul' and how is your own quest for salvation going? I mean you have been here as long as I have, and I haven't seen Jesus come down to sweep you up to Heaven yet."

Jackson responded. "Martin. You are doomed to remain here until you repent your homosexuality and wicked ways."

Martin responded. "Jackson. You are so full of shit… you are pulsating brown."

"Della... sweetie... do you want to join up with Jackson's tragic band of wingnuts or remain here with the Pink Lady party crowd?" asked Martin.

"Jackson, you may wish to soften your approach..." Martin continued, "...even the Jehovah Witnesses knock first. Why don't you just leave a magazine and we'll get back to you."

Jackson's voice responded so loud and close it made me vibrate a little bit, and not in a good way. "Della. Join us. It is your only hope for salvation! Your only hope!"

I really just wanted to get back to my interrupted psychic exchange with Bruno. "Um," I stammered, followed by a similarly vague "Umm..."

I finally gathered my thoughts and was able to speak somewhat coherently. "Jackson, is it? I appreciate your concern for me and I, umm.... think that... I... umm... well... I really don't know what um... I umm..... and I am really happy for the moment where I am but I... umm... can certainly be in touch if I um..."

I then heard Jackson's voice drop a few decibels. "Oh forget it! If you don't want out of this evil existence... then fine, be a sinner. SINNER! SINNER!" His voice was now joined by a host of other voices emanating from a newly formed crowd of glowing blue balls. All of them yelling "SINNER! SHAME! SINNER SHAME!"

Suddenly, I heard Daphne's voice's rise above the others with a power I had not heard before. "JACKSON! If you are not out of here in the next few moments, you will definitely be sorry. I can and will suck the energy out of you and every one of your band of blue balls until you pop. Is that what you want? Go try and strike fear into the hearts of true sinners. I am sure you can find other souls to save far, far away from here."

"Fine!" Jackson responded. His voice sounded like that of an angry child who had just had his favorite toy taken away. "But don't come crying to me when you are ravaged by the fires of Hell."

"The only Hell I have experienced since I have been here is your incessant ravings. I can't imagine anything worse than listening to you for all eternity. Now GET OUT OF HERE!" Daphne yelled. Suddenly, Daphne seemed to somehow expel energy from her center which made the blue balls jettison out in every direction, reminding me of a cue ball breaking up the table in a game of pool.

"That was weird," I said with a sigh of relief.

"You have no idea grrrl," stated Martin. "It's like our very own version of Jerry Falwell Live up here in Energy Ball Land."

"Daphne," I asked, "What was that little trick you did? How did you disperse them like that?"

"To tell you the truth Della," Daphne responded, "I'm not sure. It's a little trick I seemed to have picked up somehow."

"And she's the only one who can do it...." Martin added, "...that I have seen anyway. But Della you probably will find that you have some tricks up your sleeve too, because you are turning into one powerful Powder Puff. The energy is virtually vibrating off of you. Are you still popping other energy balls?"

"Not if I can help it," I responded. "However, I did accidentally suck all the energy out of that little energy ball who was always singing those old John Denver tunes."

"Oh you mean Larry from Laguna? He was kind of annoying anyway, so I can't fault you for that one. Besides, I loathe John Denver."

"No one loathes John Denver," Daphne responded. "He was a legend. How can you say anything bad about someone who wrote 'Sunshine on My Shoulders' and 'Thank God I'm A Country Boy'? Those are classics." Daphne then started humming 'Sunshine on My Shoulders', much to Martin's dismay.

"Stop It! I can't stand that song! Daphne, don't think I won't sick Miss Thing here on you. Word on the street is she is a force to be reckoned with."

"Oh Martin," I responded. "You are one funny guy. Daphne, if you could stop singing that, it would make me happy too. I much prefer 'Take Me Home Country Roads'. That one is a true classic." Daphne and I then started a loud enthusiastic rendition of 'Take Me Home.'

"NOOOOOO!" Martin screamed jokingly, "I wish someone would take ME home and away from you crazy off-key bitches!" Daphne and I ceased our singing not because of Martin's request but because we could not contain our laughter.

Once the laughter ceased, Martin added "Now, if you want to sing Madonna…that's good music"

"Well, I'm certainly not going to sing 'Like A Virgin' to you" Daphne responded as we all erupted in laughter once again.

Eleven

After my experience with Jackson and his band of not-so-merry evangelicals, I must admit that I did start to wonder a little more about what was happening to me and if, perhaps, there was something beyond where I currently found myself. With the exception of my brief and not too serious foray into Buddhism, I still believed myself to be at my very core, a Christian, and at least genetically a Catholic.

Before my father's death and prior to her hopping aboard the New Age bandwagon bound for glory, my mother had been a fairly regular churchgoer. She had instilled in us throughout our childhood and well into adulthood that despite its rules, prejudices and sometimes outlandish outfits, the Church still had some good messages to relay based on Jesus' teachings.

She insisted that despite everything else, Jesus' teachings were about love and respect for others and that we should all attempt to do as much good in this world as we could and we would be rewarded in the afterlife.

"That little voice you hear that tells you the right thing to do, that warns you just before you do something you know is wrong," she often would tell us, "That is the voice of Jesus." Through my many trials and tribulations in life, I heard that voice often. Strangely, my inner voice had a whiney New York accent to it and sounded a lot less like my idea of Jesus, and a whole lot more like Woody Allen.

I generally respected everyone's beliefs and certainly, unlike Jackson, did not think I had a monopoly on "the Truth." However, I had not read the Bible in many years and only sporadically went to church. Most of my church visits were precipitated by deaths, baptisms, weddings or in some cases merely by the desire to retreat into a refuge where I could find peace.

Up until the point of my death, I had always assumed I would see a bright light, experience a feeling of peace and be welcomed into Heaven by Jesus or at least by one of his buddies. Perhaps, that was still just around the bend. Perhaps, my faith was being tested. Perhaps, this was only a temporary stop-off on my way to the Heavenly Kingdom. Then again, perhaps it was all a load of bull cocky and this was going to be as good as it gets. In either case, I still hoped there was something beyond. If there was, I could not wait to see it. If there wasn't, things were really not all that bad here as long as I had my friends.

I had my deepest religious discussions with Kelly Sue, the Pink Lady from Nashville who despite, the current state of affairs, still clung to her Southern Methodist Christian beliefs. "This is just a test for us Della," she emphasized, "We do not know and cannot understand what God has planned for us, but we must continue to believe that the path we are on is the one we were destined to follow. I believe we are doing God's work when we help the souls here communicate with those who are still living and help those poor human souls who wish to reach those who have passed. We can choose to accept or reject a personal relationship with Him. By accepting that relationship and doing his work, we are guaranteed a place in Heaven. "

I asked her what she thought about Jackson and his evangelical energy ball contingent. "Jackson, my dear is like a rooster," Kelly Sue explained. "He is the type of man my mama used to say, thinks the sun comes up just to hear him crow. He may have seen the light at one point but now he thinks he controls the sunrise. We should pray for him."

The other Pink Ladies had an assortment of views as well. Bo Mi, who was a real Buddhist, told me that I should just believe in love and all that I really had was this moment. "Be happy in this moment," she advised "and the rest will take care of itself." Meriem, who was a Muslim, told me that she believed we would one day be reunited with our physical bodies and judged for our actions. "For now," she advised, "we are in a holding period, but you seem like you were a good woman. I think you will be OK." Debbie, who had been raised in a small evangelical church in Kentucky summarized up her religious interpretation of her current predicament with the statement, "That Jackson reminds me of my own Daddy. He thought he knew the truth but dang, I think he was way off!"

Daphne's religious perspective was quite different. "Who knows? Who cares? And what difference does it make anyway?" She felt that since there was no way of truly knowing what the future held, it was a waste of time and energy to devote too much thought to it.

Martin's viewpoint was "Baby, if Jackson and his posse are what the people in Heaven are going to be like, I will look forward to spending time in Hell with the other sinners. I am sure that is where all the fun people will be anyway."

As I stated previously, I was still uncertain myself, but I still held on to my belief in Heaven. Maybe, it was due to the way I was brought up. Maybe I knew it was true deep down in my soul. At any rate, I still looked forward to Heaven and considered this just another stop along the way. I felt like this journey was necessary and probably for reasons I did not yet understand.

Twelve

It wasn't too long before my religious ponderings were interrupted by someone calling my name in the distance. It took a few moments before I realized it was my mother's voice. My mother Helen had been a relatively quiet woman most of her life and had eschewed drinking and smoking. Until my father's death and her New Age rebirth, she had really spoken very little. She had lived an existence that centered on housework, cooking, her children, her husband and seemingly trying to be as unobtrusive to the world around her as possible.

Along with my mother's new increase in volume and confidence came a new affinity for marijuana and wine and a voice that was unlike the hesitant soft voice I had heard most of my childhood. Her voice now had both a raspy yet relaxed quality to it. I assume this vocal change was due at least in part to her new affinity for wine and marijuana.

Her voice now reminded me of the type of woman who might sit next to you at a slot machine smoking Virginia

Slims and telling you how she just won $5000 playing penny slots. Could you watch her machine while she went to the ladies room? Also, could you make sure you ordered her another White Russian if the cocktail waitress came by when she was gone.

"Della. Can you hear me? This is your mother! I miss you so much. Can you sense all of us? We are all here together now. "

Apparently, for some reason, despite my telepathic celebrity status and ability to hear them, I could not directly communicate with my family. My mental responses, however, were quickly captured by Psychic Suzie who apparently was my only conduit to the other side.

"Della, we are all here together. Your friend Penny revealed to us the story behind your unrest. We know about the money, the sweater and the guilt you have carried all these years. We are all here to say goodbye, resolve this issue once and for all and to set your soul free. I have with me your mother who flew in from Florida, your sister-in-law Janet, your best friend Penny and your old friend and coworker Cindy Benson who was kind enough to join us to address these unresolved issues."

"Don't forget Barry!" my mother's raspy voice interjected. "Animals are very sensitive to psychic phenomena. Della loved her little Barry. I can tell from his vibrations that he is sensing something unusual."

"Are you sure he just doesn't need to pee?" I heard my old friend Penny's voice jokingly add. Until I heard her voice, I had forgotten how much I had missed my best friend. Perhaps, and it made me feel guilty thinking it, I missed her more than my mother.

"Laugh all you want but animals are very sensitive and they help to pool the collective psychic energy", my mother reprimanded her.

I heard my little baby Barry bark several times.

"See there. He senses her energy." My mother's voice confirmed.

"Shhhh." Psychic Suzie warned, "We don't want to lose the connection with her. I can hear her and she is with us. She is working very hard to communicate."

"For the love of Jesus," I thought, "I didn't say anything. This is unbelievable."

"She is saying something," Suzie added, "She is speaking of Jesus and love and that this is all beyond comprehension."

"Well," I thought, "She is pretty good after all... although not technically accurate."

"If any of you have any messages you would like to convey, this is the time to do so. Cindy, we will have you speak to Della last as we want to wait to address the key issue that Della has struggled with in the afterlife. Helen, as her mother, would you like to speak first?"

My mother began. Her speech was interrupted at various points with small sobs. "Della. You have always been and will always be my baby. I remember your warm smile and strong spirit from the time you exited my womb and we welcomed you to this world. I cannot express the level of sadness that Kellen and I felt at your passing. I hope you are at peace and are spending time with your father who loved you more than anything. I feel your energy so strong and vibrant in the room today and want to let you know that you can let go my dear. We love you but want you to be free. Free to be with Jesus, the goddess or whatever celestial being is waiting for you. I will always love you and look forward to seeing you again someday. I regret that we were not as close at the end of your life as we should have been, but I have always loved you and always will. Be at peace my dear. Be at peace."

Her eloquent speech concluded with a series of sobs and sniffs. Although her speech was heartfelt, I could not help but feel it was somewhat augmented by her newfound interest in community theater.

Regardless, I felt emotion overcome me and felt a surge of love for my mother run through my being. "Please tell my mother that I love her so much and appreciate all she has done for me. I hope that her life will be happy and if Kellin makes her happy, that makes me happy. Please tell her that I will always remember our conversations and I'll always treasure our times at the beach together, picking seashells and talking about life. I would never have been the woman I came to be without her as my strength, my rock, my anchor. I owe her everything."

Psychic Suzie apparently providing the Cliff Notes version of my psychic transmission simply said "She says she loves you very much and is sending an image of seashells. Does that mean anything to you?"

"She did hear us. Oh my child." my mother exclaimed, "Kellin and I performed a goddess water ritual on the beach just before I left in her honor. The sage we burned to honor her spirit was arranged in seashells!"

"OK. That works." I thought. Clearly, this psychic stuff was not an exact science.

"Janet, you're up next", Suzie prompted.

"Well Della. I know you know how much your brother and I and little Jason miss you and want you to be at peace. We'll do anything no matter the time and expense to make sure you are free. We love you Della. That's all I have to add." Janet concluded.

"Penny, you're next" Psychic Suzie advised. "Use this time to let Della know anything that is in your heart."

"Okie dokie!" Penny replied. "Well, Della. If you can hear me and I'm not sure you can because as you know I am a little skeptical of all this hocus pocus stuff. But, on the off chance this is on the level, I want you to know you were the best friend a girl could have. We had so many good times... lots of laughs, lots of drinks and lots of memories. I hope you are in a better place. At least, I hope it's better than Hartford. I am hoping Heaven is a lot more like Hawaii. However, if not for Hartford, we would never have gotten to be such close friends so I guess the city is not completely crappy. I miss you though and really wish I knew if this was just a bunch of bullshit or if you could really hear me. If you're really out there, send us a sign. Something that will really let us know you hear us. It doesn't have to be anything crazy... just something so we know you're there. If you could wire like $40,000 to my bank account, that would be acceptable." Penny chuckled that unmistakable cackle I had grown to love.

That was Penny. Forthright and to the point with a little bit of sarcastic humor. I really wanted to let Penny know that this was all real. Although I did not know all the answers, I did know that I was dead and I could hear them. I tried to really concentrate to give them some sign... any sign... that I could hear them and that the psychic messages were not completely made up by Suzie. I concentrated and tried to manifest something... anything.

Suddenly, the unmistakable disembodied voice of Siri stated "Playing Barry Manilow." And then the lovely golden tones of Barry Manilow filled the air with a rousing rendition of "Copa Cabana".

"Holy Shit!" Penny exclaimed. "She is here! She can hear us! Barry Manilow is playing on my iPhone."

"Maybe it is just coincidental" my allegedly New Age mother said. "Maybe you bumped it or something!"

"No way!" Penny said. "This is definitely her! It is definitely her!"

"How can you be sure?" quizzed my now newly skeptical mother.

"First of all," Penny exclaimed, "I don't have any Barry Manilow songs on my phone. And secondly, if I did, I wouldn't pick that one. And most importantly, Copa Cabana is her favorite Barry Manilow song." With that, Penny completely broke down into a series of sobs, something I had never heard her do before. I am not sure if she wept for me or because her entire world view had now been turned upside down since she now realized some of this hocus pocus crap was actually real.

Thirteen

I must commend Psychic Suzie on maintaining composure during Penny's meltdown, especially since it had been preceded by Penny's derision of the psychic world and pretty much Psychic Suzie's whole chosen career path. It must have made Suzie feel good though. Perhaps, she could get a testimonial from Penny after this was all done. Maybe something to the effect of "I thought this whole psychic thing was a crock of shit, but now I am a believer." My world once again affected by the magnificent Barry Manilow.

"Well," Suzie continued, "Cindy… now it is your turn. As we spoke about, we received information from Della that she has brought with her to the other side, guilt for not admitting that she had found your two hundred twenty five dollars in the bathroom at McAllister's and then lied about it. She has told us she cannot be free unless this sin is acknowledged and forgiven."

This had seriously gone too far. I felt guilty about it but I knew I could totally move on without reliving it, whatever "moving on" meant anyway. As guilty as I still felt, I could definitely bear the burden. I mean it's not like I was actually in the room with all of them. I was just psychically connected and could psychically disconnect whenever I wanted. Besides, Cindy was such a sweet person. I am sure she would forgive me and then we could all move on.

I remembered Cindy from our McAllister days. She was impossibly beautiful in that naturally blonde, incredibly popular, perpetually sweet, unbelievably buxom and totally perfect way. Sure, she was broke like the rest of us, but she had no shortage of male suitors willing to provide her food, shelter and continual attention.

Surprisingly, Cindy's voice had not sweetened over the years and her Boston accent had become even more pronounced along with a surprisingly shall we say "colloquial" way of speaking.

"So heah's the thing." she began. "Not for nothing but that was a wicked crappy thing for Della to do to me. I mean yeah, I got the money and everything eventually, but still it, you know, really fucked up my trust with people. Della, I don't mean to like be a bitch or anything, but I mean you kind of owe me for fucking with me like that. I mean I know you're dead and all and you can't move on until I say that I forgive ya but I think you owe me somethin'. I mean not the money but somethin', you know. And that was pretty fuckin cool with the cell phone shit. Man... I mean that was awesome."

So, apparently Cindy went directly from being a waitress at McAllister's to being a stripper or possibly a dock worker. She spoke like she just got off the set of a Boston version of My Cousin Vinny. What the hell happened to her? She didn't speak that way when we worked together. I guess time can change everything including your accent!

"So heah's the thing." she continued, "My husband has been like a number one A-hole. I mean I am planning on leaving but I ain't got the money yet and I'm gonna have another kid coming out of me in like seven months or so. But he's just a total dick... you know what I mean? I want to keep the house cuz that's where me and the kids are gonna live but I know he ain't gonna just give it to me. I mean, he used to be an OK guy, but now he friggin' yells at me and the kids all the time and comes home drunk as a skunk most nights. Can't hold down a job. Just a real big A. I know I ain't the perfect mother but I love my kids and I want what's best for them. But now that I see what you can friggin' do, I was thinking if you could like scare the shit out of him and tell him to do right by me, he probably will just leave like the wuss he is and everything would be copacetic. If you could just scare the shit out of him, I could totally forgive you and we'd be good. What do you think Della?"

Everything went silent. I could just picture my mother mortified if not by Cindy's bizarre request, then by her lack of language skills. I was quite sure that Penny was contemplating how this woman and I had ever been friends. Then again, Penny was probably still reeling from the cell phone party trick.

Did Cindy really use the word "copacetic? " That was what we used to call a twenty dollar word in a speech that was probably otherwise only worth about forty-two cents.

How on earth had I gotten into this? There was no way on earth I was going to haunt her husband and was not even sure it was possible. I didn't even know how I made the cell phone play Barry Manilow in the first place. Although, I must admit I liked it and had hoped to hear the whole song. Of course, Penny had stopped it shortly after is started. Maybe, if playing Barry Manilow songs could scare her husband, I might be game, but we would have to agree to have the songs play in their entirety.

"Della says she will try but it has to be on her terms." Psychic Suzie stated firmly.

What? There goes Psychic Suzie paraphrasing again.

"And…" added Psychic Suzie just to make sure she had not lost her business sense, "it will require a medium to help facilitate the encounter and that will be at additional expense."

Psychic Suzie apparently, in addition to her psychic abilities, had not forgotten that this psychic business could be a lucrative venture. I couldn't fault her for that. Everyone needs to make a living and I bet she probably did not have a retirement plan.

"If it will help set Della free, Daniel and I will be happy to foot the bill," Janet offered.

"Kellin and I will help in any way possible as well," my mother added.

"Make sure you get all of it on film," Penny added.

"Holy crap" I thought. Here I was being psychically extorted and all my family and friends were on board. Well, I didn't really have any other plans, and if the husband really was an asshole, maybe it could be fun.

"Friggin' awesome!" Cindy yelled. "Let's gets stahted as soon as possible."

Barry barked his agreement in three short barks.

Fourteen

The Pink Ladies were fascinated with my story and were continually asking me questions about both the most recent psychic experience as well as the potential for me to engage in "haunting" activities. None of the Pink Ladies had been involved in anything resembling a haunting but were pretty confident that it could be done.

Daphne encouraged me to take mental notes and relay them back to the Pink Ladies so they could learn from the experience, if the "experience" ever happened. Martin was all excited about how I might approach the haunting and wondered if there was any way he could take part as well. Kelly Sue thought a haunting would be in bad taste but if I was going to follow through with it, it should be carefully planned and carried out with precision and careful attention to detail. Most of the other Pink Ladies thought it might be great fun if I was able to actually do carry through with it.

Marlene, the truck driver from Ottawa thought I should "definitely scare the crap out of the punk." Bo Mi, the homemaker from China warned about me using up all my energy as it seemed like this would be quite a feat. "Be careful," she warned in a heavy Asian accent, "remember you can use all your energy and disappear." It still astonished me that regardless of their ethnicity, I still heard everyone in English. I know Bo Mi did not speak English but somehow this crazy environment translated her speech in my head not only to English but to English with a Chinese accent. Weird. Perhaps, I heard the accent I expected to hear.

I heeded Bo Mi's advice and continued to drain energy out of other energy balls in exchange for psychic connections, or attempts at psychic connections with their loved ones. I built up my energy reserves and really felt more electric than I had ever felt. Red Bull had nothing on this!

I was not sure when or if my "haunting" activities would begin and I had no idea how to even start. However, it was not too long before I heard the sound of Psychic Suzie calling me. Apparently, Suzie had set up a session in Cindy's home to see what might be accomplished. Janet, Suzie, Cindy and Penny were all there. My dog Barry was conspicuously absent. We had gotten pretty good at connecting psychically by this point so I felt almost like I was there.

"Where is that ass-wipe of a husband anyway?" I heard Penny ask. "Won't he be pissed off if he finds us all camping out here in your house?"

"He won't be back for hours," Cindy responded. "He is out drinkin' with his buddy Antony. I told him me and my friends were having a sex toy pahty. That's enough to scare him away for hours. I put the kids in the bedroom to watch TV so they shouldn't be botherin' us. Let's get on with this shit. This is going to be friggin' awesome."

"Oh my," was all Janet said. I could picture her face turning the perfect shade of red although I, of course, could not see her.

"A sex toy party?" my mother said, "that sounds like fun! Kellin and I could use some new techniques." I could not believe that my seventy-one-year old mother was interested in sex toys or that she was even having sex. It also was a bit bothersome that someone who qualified for a senior discount at Denny's probably had more sex in her seventies than I had in my forties. I did my best to get it out of my mind.

Psychic Suzie interrupted, "Della has indicated she would like to get started." For once, Psychic Suzie was accurate with the message transmission. "Let's start by seeing if we can get Della to manifest herself in some way. The cell phone at our last session was good but let's see if Della can move an object. Della, I have placed a pen on the table. Can you move the pen for us?"

Despite my psychic connection, I could not see anything and certainly could not see the actual pen on the table to visualize what it looked like, or for that matter what the actual table or the actual Psychic Suzie looked like.

I concentrated and repeated "Move the pen. Move the pen. Move the pen" in my head while trying to visualize a pen on a table moving. I felt completely unsuccessful but then I heard a high pitched squeal. Did I do it?

However, the squeal was followed by Cindy yelling "Get back in the friggin' bedroom and watch TV! I told you not to bother us! Not for nuttin but if you come out of the bedroom one more time, it'll be friggin' Cheerios instead of pizza for dinner. Get back in there now!" The squealing stopped.

"OK." Suzie said, "Let's try something different. Helen, did you bring something from Della's childhood as I asked? Childhood is the most psychically aware time of everyone's existence and it makes the psychic connection stronger."

"I did." My mother stated. "I brought her Strawberry Dumpling doll. She loved that doll and wouldn't go anywhere without it when she was little. She kept it all these years." My mother's raspy voice started to sound a little weepy. "My poor little girl."

She was right. I had loved that doll. I had kept it all these years and had still even talked to the doll on occasion when I felt lonely, depressed or nostalgic and when my dog Barry was not in the mood to listen. It was a little strange I know but, hey, we all have our things. Although it had lost its scent many years ago, the doll used to blow you a strawberry scented kiss when you pressed her stomach. I also had one of her sister dolls 'Apple Crisp' but Strawberry Dumpling was definitely the queen of my doll kingdom. She had red hair and freckles and looked a little like the love child of Ronald McDonald and Lucille Ball with a sort of Little House on the Prairie hat and an apron.

"Della," Suzie stated, "Please visualize this doll from your childhood and see if you can move the doll just a bit. "

I didn't need any help visualizing the doll as it now was all I could think about. I remembered the sweet, albeit somewhat artificial, smell of strawberry. I could see myself playing with her. My fondest memory was how I would place her on the table and make her dance while singing to her. So cute! The dance would always finish with me hugging her and my reward was her blowing a sweet strawberry scented kiss.

"Holy shit!" Penny yelled, "The damn doll is dancing! This is freaking me right the hell out."

"Friggin' cool" giggled Cindy, "It's like one of those dolls from the horror movies. Can we give her a knife and have her stab my friggin' dirt bag of a husband? Not to kill him… just to fuckin freak him out. Holy crap!"

"Holy fish sticks," I heard Janet exclaim. Perhaps the closest she could come to swearing.

"This is unbelievable!" My mother added. "And I smell strawberries too!"

"Very good work, Della" Suzie stated calmly. "Can you make the lights flicker now?"

The more I visualized my little doll, the more powerful I became. At Suzie's request I was able to make the lights flicker, was able to make the doll rise off the table and float in midair, and perform a number of other psychic tasks. Hearing all the gasps and exclamations, I got so caught up in the excitement I couldn't stop! It was such fun!

I pictured myself and Strawberry Dumpling dancing and playing. I could almost see the doll's smiling face as I continued to make her tap her little doll feet on the table. I visualized myself holding her and both of us twirling around the room faster and faster. I laughed and experienced a childlike joy that I had not felt in ages! Suddenly, I felt dizzy and then there was a tremendous "pop." The doll apparently collapsed on the table, the lights went out, and then someone screamed just before my mind went blank.

Fifteen

The first thing I remember after the darkness lifted was actually seeing a bunch of faces and eyes looking down at me in a foggy haze. I felt like I was on an operating room table with the doctors and nurses trying to decide if the organ transplant took.

"Is it dead?" I heard Penny's unmistakable voice ask. As the group of peering eyes came into focus, I recognized them as the eyes of Penny, my mother, my sister-in-law, an overweight and acne-ridden Cindy Benson, and a pretty face with beautiful blue eyes that must have belonged to Psychic Suzie.

"I think Della must have experienced a psychic overload." Suzie stated. "I think we have lost the connection for now."

"That was friggin unbelievable" Cindy exclaimed. "If we can have the doll do that for my husband, he would be totally freaked. Can we get her to moan 'Leave this goddamn house you asshole' or something like that?"

"I think we have done enough for today," Psychic Suzie replied. "We will need one more session and then we will see what we can do regarding the haunting. Della will need to replenish her energy and we'll connect with her again, perhaps tomorrow."

"Same time, same place?" Cindy offered.

"If that works for everyone, it works for me." Suzie answered.

"I'll bring back the doll tomorrow," my mother offered.

"I'm completely freaked out," Penny added.

The eyes backed away and I felt the sensation of rising in the air, the light dimming and then and I was in almost total darkness. I could see very little but could see the dim outline of various objects and could smell the unmistakable smell of marijuana which I had always detested. As I investigated my hazy surroundings, I realized what had happened. My spirit had somehow possessed my Strawberry Dumpling doll and I was currently confined to my mother's purse. Despite her age, my mother continued to smoke pot although I am sure she would say it was solely for medicinal use. If I wasn't careful, Strawberry Dumpling and I could get a contact high. In addition, I saw the outline of a gun.

What in the world was my New Age mother doing with a gun? Who was this woman?

I heard my mother getting into a taxi and then the next thing I knew, I heard a door unlocking and the sound of barking. "Shhhh…" my mother's voice warned, "Barry! Quiet down now!" I felt something tugging at my mother's bag.

"Barry. No. Bad boy. Now go lie down," my mother warned. Barry barked a few more times. "Barry. It is hard enough to find a hotel that will take dogs. If you continue, we'll be barred from La Quinta for life. Please leave my bag alone."

Suddenly, I felt the sensation of a cold nose pressed against my skin and two happy eyes peering down at me.

"Barry," I said to myself. "My baby. It is so good to see you."

Barry's face had come into full focus now. He cocked his head to the left and then to the right and whimpered a little bit while continuing to stare directly at me.

"Leave the doll alone now," my mother cautioned. I then felt myself being lifted and placed on what must have been a desk or dresser. I continued to feel Barry's eyes staring at me quizzically. "That was your Mommy's

favorite doll. Now I will not allow you to chew on it."
Barry continued to stare for what seemed like hours.

The unmistakable smell of marijuana filled the air and
from the corner of my vision I saw my mother appear and
reappear smoking what was clearly a joint. When she
finished smoking, I heard the sound of spritzing and my
mother repeating the phrase "Febreze... do your magic!"

Barry continued to stare at me without moving his gaze
for a moment.

"My sweet little man," I thought. "I wish I could give
you a great big hug."

Barry's head cocked to the left once again and he
whimpered. I was beginning to think he could hear me.
Every time I said something in my mind, he cocked his
head as if understanding.

The next thing I knew Barry had jumped extremely
high, grabbed me by my Strawberry Dumpling body and
started running around the room with me in his mouth.
My clearly stoned and exasperated mother chased after
him.

"Will you please drop the doll?" my mother yelled.
She managed to corner Barry in the space between the
window and the bed. "Put it down!" she shouted again.

Barry looked at her for a moment and then jumped onto the bed and over the other side, just escaping her grasp. Barry then ran into the bathroom. My mother quickly followed him and shut the door blocking any avenue of escape. Barry backed up towards the walk-in shower maintaining a firm grip on my doll body. My mother managed to get hold of the doll's feet and tried to pull the doll from Barry's grip. Barry growled playfully but would not relinquish his prize. My mother, perhaps fearing the doll would be damaged, released her grip and glared angrily at Barry.

She then lowered the toilet seat, sat down, folded her arms and continued to glare at Barry. "Fine. I can wait here all night until you decide to drop it." Barry gazed back at her with the look that clearly said, "And so can I old woman... so can I."

Eventually, I managed to communicate to Barry, "Drop it!" Perhaps, I should have said "Drop me!" Barry hesitated for a moment and then obeying my order deposited the doll on the bathroom floor. My mother heaved a sigh of relief, collected up my doll body and placed me on a shelf in the closet and shut the closet door, leaving me in complete darkness. I later heard her shut the hotel room door and leave with Barry. I was left alone for quite some time.

Was this now my destiny? Was my energy ball phase over and now I was destined to inhabit a thirty-five year old Strawberry Dumpling doll? Were my Pink Lady days at an end? At the very least, I was dressed in pink!

I still felt it was not implausible that Jesus or his second in command might show up at any second, commend me for my patience and then lead me to paradise. However, although I thought it plausible, it did not seem very likely. I also thought maybe I would wake up and all of this would have been a dream. Perhaps, I had just been knocked out during the accident and all the events to date were a product of my overactive imagination. This, I told myself, was unlikely too. My imagination had never been this crazy!

Sixteen

I remained in complete darkness for what seemed like an eternity. For a while I heard my mother talking to herself, talking to the dog, talking on the phone and singing what I can only describe as a sexually explicit version of "This Land is Your Land." I will leave it up to your imagination but it is not a version of the song you ever want to hear your elderly mother sing. Eventually, I tuned out my mother's voice and her off-color versions of popular patriotic tunes and settled into a semi-meditative state in the complete darkness that surrounded me.

Suddenly my catatonic state was interrupted by a brilliant white light and what I could only think must be the singing of angels. It turned out my mother had just opened the closet door with what turned out to be a CD of Susan Boyle singing "How Great Thou Art." Of course, after a few minutes, my mother's off-key singing joined in, which dissolved any further illusion of beatific intervention. Once she stopped singing, I heard my mother's voice state clearly, "Well, Dumpling this is your big day!" followed by a cacophony of coughing, wheezing and choking. I was not sure if this was the result of a "wake and bake" or if her vocal chords were rebelling after her attempts to hit Ms. Boyle's high notes. At any rate, before long we were in transit back to another episode of "Psychic Suzie Resurrects Strawberry Dumpling."

I must admit although I still did feel bad about the whole Cindy Benson money fiasco, I was starting to feel a little like a psychic prostitute and was less and less inclined to participate in this cockamamie "haunt my asshole husband" adventure. I decided before we entered Cindy's house that both Strawberry Dumpling and I would be keeping our traps shut and our dancing feet still. Hopefully, my mother would follow our lead and keep her singing and hacking under control as well.

I won't get into all the details of our next psychic session but basically Psychic Suzie, my mother, Janet and Cindy pleaded with me to give them a sign that I was present, to make the doll move again, to flicker the lights or to provide any evidence that I was there. I did nothing and tried to tune them out as best I could.

"Well," Psychic Suzie said with a sigh, "It looks like Della is not up for this today. I sense her presence but perhaps her energy levels were depleted yesterday and we may need to reschedule in a few days."

"Thank God!" Penny exclaimed. "I didn't sleep at all last night. Every time I fell asleep, all I kept seeing was Strawberry Dumpling climbing up the side of the bed with a knife, a crazy look in her eyes and the smell of rotten fruit on her breath. I don't think my nerves could handle it. Della if you are out there… can you find some way other than a creepy dancing doll to let us know? Thanks hon."

"This is bullshit!" I heard Cindy yell. "I want this fuckin' doll to do something creepy and scare the shit out of my husband. You need to make it talk too. It needs to have a creepy voice and tell the dickweed he needs to leave."

The more I thought about this stupid plan, I could not believe all of these relatively sane people had bought into it. I mean seriously, this was to be my penance for inadvertently stealing money? Well, Cindy could go suck eggs. I was ready to go back to energy ball land and hang out with people who really appreciated me.

Psychic Suzie tried to calm Cindy down. "Now Cindy, this is not an exact science. We cannot control what those who are in a different plane are willing to do or able to do. I am getting the feeling that Della no longer feels like this is a good idea. Perhaps, you can just tell her you forgive her and let her spirit be released."

"No effen way!" responded Cindy. "The only release I want is a release from my goddamn marriage. Gimme the damn doll."

"No" I heard my mother yell. "You can't have it. That was Della's favorite childhood toy. She loved that doll and would never forgive me if anything happened to it. Give it back!"

"Well since she is goddamn dead, she doesn't need the goddamn doll. I'm taking it. If I can't get a freakin' haunting out of this. I am taking the stupid doll and making some money. I'll make the goddamn thing dance again. If this two-bit snake chahmah here can't do it, I'll find someone who can. Besides, I got part of that whole dancing doll shit on my cell phone video. "

"You are being very rude!" Suzie responded in utter shock. "And you can't make Della do anything she doesn't want to. You should not have recorded any part of that session without permission. That is blatantly against the law."

"Bite me." I heard Cindy respond. Next think I know, Cindy and I were on a mad dash out the door and I was thrown face up on what I presume to be the front seat of

Cindy's car. I use the term 'car' loosely because it appeared to be something from an episode of Hoarders. The place was a mish-mash of all kinds of random things. Burger wrappers, troll dolls, aluminum cans, piles of papers, plastic flowers and a surprisingly intact bobble head of former President Reagan filled my peripheral vision. The car had a strange odor that seemed to be a combination of cigarettes, pine air freshener, body odor and car exhaust.

"All right, Dolly baby... we are going to hit the big time now!" Cindy yelled. I heard the simultaneous squeal of tires and what I hoped was the backfiring of the car. I was worried it could have been my mother shooting at the car as I now knew she carried a small pistol in her purse. The noises were quickly supplanted by the unmistakable, calming and unforgettable melodies of AC/DC.

Seventeen

Needless to say, Cindy was not the brightest bulb in the basket and I wondered if she had forgotten that she had not only left the whole psychic gang back at her own house but also had left her kids. She would certainly not be winning any Mother of the Year awards.

We were probably only ten minutes into our journey, when I saw blue lights reflected in the car's interior and AC/DC being interrupted by the tell-tale sound of a police car siren. This was also accompanied by Cindy's repeated, repetitive and surprisingly creative use of the F-word.

Although on the few occasions I had been stopped by a police officer for speeding, I would break out in a sweat, pull my car over immediately and seemingly lose my ability to speak, this was not the case with Cindy. She only pulled over when I heard the police officer announcing through a loudspeaker, "Ma'am, pull your car over NOW! This is not a joke!"

I felt the car slow down and eventually it came to a stop with an audible sigh from Cindy accompanied by a relatively benign "Goddammit." She switched off the blasting AC/DC music.

After a few minutes, an officer appeared at the driver's window. "Ma'am, I am Officer Harold Jacobsen from the Quincy Police Department. When a police officer indicates that you should pull over, you need to pull over immediately. Is there a reason why it took you over a mile to do so?"

Cindy's voice changed from her normal hardened vulgarity-laden tone to a voice which sounded much more like the relatively innocent college girl I knew. "I am so sorry officer. I did not realize you were following me. Was I doing something wrong? If I was, I am so sorry. "

"Sure," the officer responded. "May I see your license and registration, please?"

"Absolutely. Just give me a minute." I could see her hands and a bunch of papers flying this way and that.

After a brief pause, Cindy responded, "Well officer, here is my license. I can't seem to locate my registration at the moment. I'll keep looking though!" This statement was punctuated by a girlish giggle. Was this the same woman who normally used the F-bomb in every sentence and blasted AC/DC? Not to mention being the ruthless kidnapper of an innocent Strawberry Dumpling doll?

"I'll be right back," the officer responded and I heard his footsteps walk away from the car. Cindy resumed muttering the F-word in various creative ways in an almost manic manner.

I heard the footsteps returning and the officer say, "Ma'am. I am going to need for you to get out of the car, please."

"What do you mean, officer?" Cindy responded in her newly minted sweet innocent voice. "I am sure I will find that darned registration if you give me a few more moments."

"Ma'am. Please step out of the car. I don't want to have to ask you again."

That was enough to snap Cindy back to her normal state. The sweet innocent voice was gone as I heard her say "Oh for fuck Christ's sake. Just give me a goddamn ticket. This is fuckin' ridiculous. I mean what the fuck... seriously?"

"Ma'am. I would advise you to refrain from using that language. Now, please step out of the car and move to the side of the road," the police officer responded somehow maintaining his cool.

I couldn't hear much of what happened next through the closed window on the passenger side but there was certainly a lot of commotion. The next thing I knew I was hearing a succession of loud beeps and the front of the car started to rise. A scruffy overweight man with a shirt bearing the ubiquitous name "Hank" fiddled with the ignition and then shifted the car into neutral gear. After burping loudly, he exited the vehicle and slammed the driver side door shut. The car was being towed.

Before too long, Cindy's face appeared in the driver-side window yelling, "Wait! I need that fuckin' doll. Give me my fuckin' doll." This was punctuated by the now clearly exasperated officer's voice. "Ma'am. I told you to get away from the car. Ma'am. Get away from the car!"

The last think I heard was Cindy's unmistakable voice yelling "Bite Me!"

Eighteen

It was a long and bumpy ride to the lot where impounded cars are stored. After a seemingly endless series of beeps emanating from the tow truck, the car was finally deposited and lowered back to the ground. Shortly after that, the driver side door opened up and the tow truck driver Hank reappeared. He was dressed in a dirty work shirt bearing his name. The shirt was stained in various places with oil and other liquids of varying colors. His navy blue pants featured similar stains as well as holes in both the knees. He was a large man whose presence seemed to fill not only the driver's compartment but to also expand into the passenger area where my Strawberry Dumpling form sat quietly staring perpetually into space. He wore a baseball cap that featured the slogan "Rough and Redneck" along with a cartoon of a man drinking a large beer. Stubble seemed to somehow cover almost all of his face and neck leaving only his forehead and the area just below his eyes free of whiskers. He smelled like sweat and what I presumed to be garlic. "What a shithole!" he proclaimed as he looked around the vehicle.

He thrust one of his large hairy arms directly in my line of vision and popped open the glove compartment. He peered into its dark recesses as he whistled a tune only known to him. He gathered up some loose change that sat in the middle driver console and then his eyes settled on me.

"Well! What have we here?" he asked himself as he lifted me up in one of his huge greasy paws. "Looks like someone left you behind little darlin'. Well, that wasn't very nice was it? I know just the place for you." He then smiled a broad smile revealing an assortment of teeth of varying shades of white, gray, black and yellow. He then continued to look in the back seat selecting various items from the large assortment of miscellaneous objects in the car and placing them in his pocket or underneath one of his arms.

"With a mess like this, I am sure she won't miss a few things!" he proclaimed and laughed softly to himself. "Rewards of the trade" he muttered and emphasized the point with a loud burp.

Hank wrapped me in a towel and deposited me in the back cab of his truck and continued to perform his daily duties. I could not see anything with the towel wrapped around me but I could hear country music blaring for the remainder of the day. Hank's deep off-key baritone voice accompanied most of the songs and what he lacked in quality, he more than made up for in volume.

Eventually, Hank unwrapped me from the towel I was encased in and sat me in the passenger seat of his truck. "Sorry to have covered you up," he apologized to me. "A man's truck is a dirty place and I don't want you getting dirty! You are going to love where I am bringing you and your new family is going to love you too! You'll see little darlin'." He laughed again softly and then turned up the radio and joined Willie Nelson in a rousing rendition of "Mamas Don't Let Your Babies Grow Up To Be Cowboys."

Hank drove through what seemed to be an endless network of dirt roads and forest until we finally arrived at his home. It was a non-descript white double-wide trailer set far back in the woods. An assortment of discarded tools and debris littered the yard. Rusted metal objects of various sizes and shapes covered the landscape... some were recognizable... some were not. An old and evidently non-functioning ride-on mower sat beside a discarded double sink whose bottom had almost completely rusted out. An abandoned toilet peeked out from the weeds and sat beside what appeared to be the remnants of a baby carriage that had seen much better days. An old rusty engine sat on a tree stump and was flanked on either side by two rusted garden rakes that had lost part of their wooden handles and had been stuck upright in the dirt.

Hank grabbed me with one hand and paused at the main door. He knocked a few times and then announced. "Girls! I have a new friend for you. You are going to love her!" He smiled and laughed softly again as he opened the door and entered.

I was expecting to see two little ragamuffin daughters run up to greet their smiling father as he presented them with another of his found treasures. However, once we entered, I realized there were no girls in sight or anyone else for that matter.

The house reeked of some sort of overly sweet cologne which infiltrated my nostrils, well perhaps not my actual doll nostrils but whatever orifice or sense allowed me to smell. The smell reminded me of a combination of Old Spice and fermenting cabbage.

The home itself was literally packed to the rafters with dolls of every imaginable shape and size. Dolls sat silently on shelves that covered every spare inch of wall space. A large Raggedy Ann doll that was perhaps four feet tall peered ominously from one dark corner. A cadre of perhaps fifty Barbie dolls in various states of dress peered from one of the shelves directly in front of the door. Porcelain dolls in elaborate outfits stared down from another shelf. A shelf full of dolls in princess outfits occupied still another shelf. Another shelf featured an assortment of baby dolls in diapers, onesies and bibs. Dolls occupied the chairs at the table in the kitchen and sat in the upholstered chairs in the living room. Dolls occupied all but one open space on the couch and several dolls were perched on swings suspended from the ceiling.

An elaborate tea set was set up around a folding table in the living room surrounded by three dolls. Here I was a dead woman occupying a doll's body and I, myself, was getting a little freaked out. I recalled vividly horror movies where dolls came to life and did hideous things. I can't imagine how freaked out a Girl Scout or Jehovah Witness would be who made the unfortunate decision to knock on Hank's door.

"Do excuse me Esmerelda" Hank announced as he picked up an elaborately dressed Victorian doll from her seat at the tea table. "Our new guest will be joining us for tea and we are just so short on seats. I am sure you won't mind." He placed me in the seat Esmerelda previously occupied and placed her beside another doll on one of the upholstered chairs. "Now ladies, I am going to shower. Please make our new guest feel at home.

I don't know her actual name but let us call her Berry since she is from the Strawberry Dumpling clan. "

"Lenora, please introduce her to the other girls," he requested, addressing a realistic looking doll with long dark hair and pretty blue eyes who was one of the remaining dolls at the table. "I am thinking Berry may be able to help in our nursery but we'll see what tasks she may be best suited for." Hank then went off to the shower and I could hear him whistling merrily above the sound of the running water.

"This is fantastic." I thought. "From the hands of a madwoman to the house of a perverted twisted tow truck driver." I didn't even want to think of what kind of sick things he did to these dolls. There were probably dismembered doll bodies in the basement.

"He is definitely strange but he is relatively harmless" an elderly woman's voice stated firmly, emanating from the doll he had addressed as Lenora. "This is not how I planned to spend my life but I guess it could be worse."

"Did you say that?" I asked of my tea party partner. "Who are you?"

"You can call me Lenora since that is what he calls me. I've almost forgotten I have had any other existence."

"Hi Lenora. My name is Della but I guess I am going to be Berry for the time being. You're trapped inside a doll's body too?" I responded.

"Oh, yes… I have been in this doll body for a number of years now. Five years at least, I think. He bought me at a flea market. This doll was one of the remaining items from my estate when I died. My daughters sold everything. I thought they might want to keep some of the old dolls in my collection, but they were not interested and considered it an old lady's folly. I always loved this doll and somehow my soul occupied it after I died."

"Were you an energy ball too? How did you come to be in the body of a doll?"

"Was I an energy what?" Lenora answered. "I'm sure I don't know what you mean, dear."

"When you died did you go to another plane of existence before you were trapped in the doll's body?"

"I don't think so," Lenora responded. "I died and floated around for a bit. I saw the doll and before I knew it I <u>was</u> the doll. Trapped for all eternity I fear. It sounds like you have a different story."

I explained to Lenora my experience with the afterworld and how my overexcited performance at a séance resulted in my current situation.

"That sounds much more exciting than my story and gives me hope that maybe I will find my way out of here. I never thought I would be living out my afterlife in a trailer in the woods with a man who thinks he is some doll-version of Clark Gable. It is certainly a strange situation but he really does treat all of the dolls very well. He just does not treat himself very well. He is delusional I fear, but harmless all the same. "

"Are you the only doll here that can speak?" I asked.

"Well, I am not sure I would call it speaking but it is communicating in some way and there seems to be three of us here in similar straits. Myself, Virginia who he keeps in the bedroom most of the time and Catherine who is up on one of the shelves. Catherine, say 'Hello' to Della if you can hear us! She is trapped just like us."

"I am just above your head Lenora," a voice responded with what seemed to be a British accent. "You can't see me but I can see you. If he would ever take me off the shelf, maybe we could have a decent conversation for once. Welcome to our little nightmare Della. Maybe, you're here to save us? "

"I don't think so," I answered. "I will certainly do my best though, should the opportunity arise."

"What I wouldn't do for a bloody drink and a gun. If I wasn't already dead, I would shoot myself but I'd be more than happy to shoot him and then destroy all the bloody dolls in this bizarre museum," Catherine responded.

"Now, Catherine it's not that bad. It could be much worse. Now, don't scare our new friend. I am sure we are all here for quite a while. We might as well make the best of it." Lenora responded.

"A woman can still dream of her liberation," Catherine responded. "Lenora, I know you collected dolls during your life so perhaps this is more of a familiar situation for you. It is a bloody nightmare for me! Dolls have always made me incredibly uncomfortable and yet here I am trapped in a doll's body. Fate is a cruel mistress."

"I'm sorry that you have ended up in this situation. Maybe, it's only temporary. How did you end up in the doll's body anyway?" I asked Catherine.

"Oh, my dear, this is only the latest stop in what appears to be a never ending cycle. When I died which seems so ever long ago in the 1920's, I found myself in a place that was so beautiful and peaceful. Then one day, poof, I found myself thrust into the body of a song sparrow."

"A song sparrow?" I asked.

"Oh, yes. A brief life to be sure. I flew into a window and broke my little neck. My spirit then inhabited a rock. Yes, I was a rock for ever so long. One does not think of a spirit being encased in a rock or a rock having a spirit at all, but there I sat for what seemed like forever. One day, I was dug up by a young man with a shovel doing some sort of construction and then I somehow merged with the young man's spirit for a time. It was a battle between his spirit and mine though and I evidently lost out and I found my spirit thrust out of him and into a book. I have also been a donkey, a flower, a mouse, a fly, a chair, a tree and now a doll. You would think with all these incarnations, I would have a clearer idea of what was happening, but alas, I do not."

"That is incredible," I responded.

"A bloody nightmare is what it is. The tree was my favorite though. I loved being a tree. Oh, how I wish I was a tree again. I hope someone will come along and free me from this capitalistic mass-produced plastic doll prison I now inhabit. I am probably stamped 'Made in China.' China. I never enjoyed that country. Too many people. Too much noise. Too much rice. I do apologize my dear as I realize I am a little bitter."

"That's all right." I answered. "We all just make it up as we go along."

"That we do," Catherine responded.

Suddenly, we heard footsteps in the hallway and Hank's whistling. "You're in for a treat now, Della," Lenora forewarned me. "It's tea time."

Nineteen

Hank emerged from the bathroom dressed in a white dress shirt, black pants, a worn suit jacket and a bright blue tie. His hair was slicked back and appeared to be coated with some sort of oil. His tie was too short and made it only half way down his enormous belly. The lower section of his tie rested horizontally across the beginning of his protruding stomach. He smiled broadly. I now knew where the sickeningly sweet cologne smell had come from as he apparently had doused himself in it. As crazy as it seemed, I much preferred the sweaty smell he reeked of when he originally took me from Cindy's car. Clearly, sweat was the lesser of the two evils and easier to handle. I wondered if my little doll eyes were watering at the stench.

"Ladies, it is time for our evening tea!" he announced as if he were the Lord of the Manor and not just the Duke of the Double-wide.

He seated himself in the empty chair at the table and adjusted the tea cups and saucers at each place setting. I sat immediately to his right, Lenora sat to his left and a painted bisque doll with a disturbing flat face that reminded me of a Chinese Pug sat across from him. He took the top off of the fancy teapot which occupied the center of the table and placed it beside the pot. He then stood up, went to the kitchen and returned with a large bottle of gin which he proceeded to pour into the ornate teapot until it was filled to the top. He placed the top back on the teapot and returned the gin to the kitchen. He returned to his seat and filled each teacup half-way with gin.

"I would like to propose a toast to our newest friend, Berry. Berry, it is so lovely that you can join us in our home and I hope you will find it comfortable here. We do have fun girls, don't we?" He raised his teacup high into the air above his head and announced "To Berry!" He held the cup not delicately by the handle in the customary way, but wrapped his enormous hand around the cup so it was barely visible and gulped down the gin in one shot.

He proceeded to swap his cup with the one he had placed in front of me and downed the contents of my cup in the same manner. He looked down at the now empty cup in front of me and stated, "Berry, you certainly drank that fast. I can see you are a little party girl. Let me refill that for you. Lenora disapproves of drinking our tea too fast so be careful or she will scold you! Only fooling Lenora!" Hank then winked at Lenora and refilled my cup with another generous pour of gin.

"Celeste, do you not want your tea, sweetie?" Hank asked looking across the table at the bisque doll who stared blankly back at him. "Well, I will just have your tea then," he responded. Hank then quickly gulped down this teacup of gin as well and returned the empty vessel to its original spot. He then refilled his own cup and this time casually sipped at it.

"Where are my manners?" he then announced. "We should have some music to accompany our tea. Shall I play or would you like to do the honors, Lenora?" Lenora, of course, stared blankly back at Hank.

"I understand Lenora, but that is a shame because you have the voice of a songbird. Well, it looks like I will be performing then!" Hank then produced a shiny harmonica from his pocket. "This is a song I wrote specifically for Celeste in honor of her birthday. I call it 'Beautiful Star' because Celeste you are like a beautiful star in the night sky."

Celeste's flattened bisque face offered him no response. If Celeste was a "beautiful star," Lenora and I were supermodels.

Hank proceeded to play an endless assortment of discordant notes which were so loud that they rattled the teacups. At various intervals, he would stop the harmonica playing and howl out a chorus consisting of the words, "Byooootiful. Byooootiful. Byooootiful star! You are a byooootiful star!" He would then gulp down another cup of gin and resume his harmonica revelry. After what felt like several long and painful hours, he finally deposited his harmonica back in his pocket and then took Celeste's little doll hand and asked "May I have this dance, my little lady?" He pressed the doll close to his chest and whirled around the room in a perverse waltz while crooning "Byootiful byooootiful star!" He ended the dance with a kiss on the doll's cheek and then announced, "I cannot leave my other ladies out!" and proceeded to dance with each of us in a similar manner, continuing to gulp down teacups full of gin in between dances. By the last dance he was wobbling noticeably. Curiously, both Lenora and I remained silent during the whole event. As for myself, I am pretty sure I was in shock.

"It is time for your prince to retire for the evening!" Hank finally slurred while emptying the last remnants of gin from the bottle into his teacup and gulping it down. "Good night, sweet Berry. Good night my regal Lenora. Good night my evening star Celeste." He bowed to each of us in sequence. He then proceeded to stumble his way around the room bidding each of the endless array of dolls good night by name. When he retired to his bedroom, I could hear him bidding the dolls there good night as well.

"Oh my," I exclaimed, finally breaking my silence. "That was something!"

"Like I said, "Lenora responded. "He is relatively harmless."

"Like I said," Catherine added from the shelf above Lenora's head, "he is a bloody wingnut."

Twenty

Hank repeated this ritual every night for what I believe was four nights. On the second night, Lenora was moved back to a shelf and another doll who Hank referred to as Isabelle took her seat. Celeste remained in her seat with the same glazed blank look on her flat face. Isabelle was a large doll with curly blonde ringlets. Hank frequently scolded her for making inappropriate comments during tea time, although I heard nothing other than Catherine's laughter from the shelf above Isabelle's head. Towards the end of our perverse tea party on the fourth night, we heard a car pull up, a car door shut and loud rapping on the door to the trailer.

Hank froze in shock, evidently not used to having visitors. "You girls just stay put. Let me take care of this," Hank spoke to us with such seriousness. Did he really think any of us were able to get up and answer the door? If we could, I am certain there would be a mass doll exodus down the dirt roads of Dolltown. Can you imagine? That would certainly freak out the townspeople!

"Who is it?" Hank called out in his deepest baritone voice, obviously intended to scare off any intruders to his perverse tea party.

I heard my sister-in-law Janet's voice respond, "Mr. Martin. We're sorry to disturb you but the garage told us we might catch you here and that you would not be back to work for several days. We are trying to locate a lost item, a doll that was left in a car that you towed. It is quite important that we get it back."

"Just a minute," Hank gruffly replied. He looked directly at me and said. "I should have known someone would be looking for a pretty little angel like you. This is trouble. Trouble with a capital T, buttercup! I'll protect you though. I won't let them take you."

Hank's large form obscured my view through the door window but I heard him say "Now, what is this all about, ladies?"

Janet responded, "As I said, I am sorry to bother you at home. My name is Janet Hampton and this is my mother-in-law Helen. Oh my, I hope we didn't catch you on your way out. I see you are dressed up..."

"Well, you did. I have a date with a young lady and I don't have a lot of time," Hank responded abruptly.

"I'll make it quick then," Janet replied. "We are searching for a doll that was in a car that you towed earlier this week. We went to retrieve the doll which has very special meaning to us. It was actually stolen by the woman whose car you towed. We are in a bit of a rush which is why we thought we would stop by your home. The folks at the garage indicated that they had not seen it and that perhaps you might have taken it. We need to find the doll as soon as possible and they told us you would not be back for several days. They were nice enough to provide us your address. Have you seen it, by chance? "

I heard my mother's voice pipe up. "It is a Strawberry Dumpling doll. It is pink with a little bonnet, a pink dress and a little apron."

"Haven't seen it," Hank responded. "Now if you don't mind, I have to go. I'm kind of in a rush."

"Here," I heard Janet's voice say. "This my name and number. If you do happen to see it, please give us a call as soon as possible."

"Sure," Hank replied. "Although, I can't imagine why finding a little old doll is so important."

"It's a family thing," I heard my mother respond. "It belonged to my deceased daughter and it has a lot of personal meaning to me and our family. And, there is a reward if you find it!"

"A reward?" Hank's interest was now apparently peaked. "How much of a reward if I did happen to find it?"

"One hundred… err… One hundred fifty dollars," I heard my mother answer.

"Really?" Hank answered with obvious interest. "Well, I will see what I can do to help you in your search. Of course, I would never have taken anything from a vehicle but sometimes some of the other guys at the yard can be less than trustworthy. Let me see what I can find out and I will give you a call if I can locate your sweet little baby."

"Yes… thank you," Janet replied with a little shakiness in her voice. She sounded a little creeped out by Hank's use of the phrase "sweet little baby" to describe the lost doll. Her voice now had that distinct quality of a woman who realized she had wandered into an environment that was far outside her comfort zone. "Please be in touch."

My mother's raspy voice, which seemed to be less freaked out than Janet's announced boldly, "That is one hundred fifty dollars, Hank. One hundred fifty dollars but we need that doll soon."

"I'll see what I can do. Now ladies, if you will pardon me, I need to get ready. Thanks for stopping by." I heard the door slam and watched Hank return to the living room. He picked me up in the air and kissed me several times. I cringed with each kiss he planted.

"You, my little blossom, are worth one hundred and fifty dollars. Now, as much as I think you are as sweet as sugar, I can use that money! So how about one last dance?" He proceeded to down a teacup of gin and twirl with me around the room. He then stopped and patted me on the back as if he intended to burp me. "I knew you were something special. I just knew it!"

Suddenly, I heard a tapping sound coming from the living room window which happened to be directly in my line of vision. At first, I thought it was a bird but then I could see that it was a pink fingernail tapping on the window, visible from the gap between the curtains. I then saw the unmistakable eyeball of my mother peering through the gap and heard her yelling "Give me the goddamn doll asshole!"

The tapping was soon supplanted by a loud banging on the door and my mother's voice now yelling ever more loudly. "I knew you had it! You crazy freak. Give me the doll! Give it to me now!"

131

Hank twirled around several times at first, not realizing what was happening. "I want the one hundred and fifty dollars!" He yelled back as he cautiously approached the door. He held me up in front of him for emphasis.

I heard my mother's voice respond. "You will get nothing. Give us the doll!"

Janet, in an unsuccessful attempt to calm my mother down pleaded with her "Helen, let's just give him the money and get on our way."

Hank cautiously opened the door and responded. "No money! No doll!"

My mother pushed herself into the entryway separating the door from the kitchen and Hank used his bulk to block her from moving further. I still shuddered in amazement at how this previously meek woman was transforming into a renegade senior citizen.

Before any of us knew what was happening, my mother had retrieved the handgun from her purse and started firing over Hank's shoulders at the various dolls that occupied the shelves in the kitchen. A porcelain head exploded. Another plastic doll careened off the shelf as a bullet made impact with it. Was this really my mother?

Damn, she was a good shot. Janet looked on in complete disbelief and genuine fear.

Hank who could have easily knocked both women aside with one arm looked on in horror. He squealed in a voice higher pitched than his normal baritone. "Stop it! Stop it! You crazy bitch! Leave my girls alone. You killed Holly!' He dropped me on the table as he went over to retrieve the plastic doll my mother had shot off her shelf. "Holly. Lovely little Holly. Are you OK?" Hank was clearly on the verge of a major display of an uncontrollable waterworks of troubling tears.

I heard Catherine calling from her shelf in the living room, "Please shoot me. Please, shoot me in the bloody heart or please take me with you." Of course, no one could hear her but me.

Lenora also pleaded, "Take us with you Della! Take us with you!"

I called back, "I would if I could! Goodbye Lenora! Catherine…I hope you will be a tree again!"

My mother quickly snatched me off the kitchen table. She then produced a digital camera and started snapping pictures of the inside of the trailer with abandon. "If you so much as come near us, I will circulate these pictures to all your buddies down at the garage. Come on Janet," my mother announced, "let's get out of here."

Janet looked at Hank and then turned and looked at my mother. She then quietly followed her from the trailer. Janet handed my mother the car keys, and sat down quietly in the passenger seat. She held me on her lap and stared blankly into space.

"More than happy to drive!" my mother exclaimed and proceeded to speed down the dirt driveway and away from Hank's Home for Wayward Dolls. Janet remained silent for the duration of the ride, obviously still in shock from her experience.

Twenty One

I have never been completely sure what happened just before I was rescued but from what I could piece together, a number of things had occurred. One, Cindy had been arrested. Two, Cindy had a number of other altercations other than doll-knapping on her record which must have contributed to her incarceration, in addition to her less than stellar performance with the police officer. Three, for some reason, my mother had agreed to post bail for Cindy. And four, and perhaps most importantly, somehow in the midst of all this Cindy had posted her video of my possessed Strawberry Dumpling doll dance routine on the Internet and it had apparently garnered a fair amount of interest.

Cindy called my mother's cell phone as we were returning to my townhouse. Cindy's voice reverberated through the car via the car's Bluetooth connection. "I appreciate you bailing me out. It was a pretty shitty thing for me to do. I know. I know. But remember our deal…

the video is mine and I had better see something out of this or... or... well... shit is going fly."

"Cindy," my mother responded. "A deal is a deal. Now, I paid the five hundred dollars for your bail and you are lucky we didn't press charges. We'll give you the credit you deserve. You have no idea what we had to go through to get the doll back. None of that would have happened if not for your shenanigans."

Cindy reminded my mother, "There would not even be a video if not for me. And I'm the one who posted it. Don't fuck me over."

"We are not going to... er... F... you over. I just want my daughter to be able to rest in peace. And if we can educate folks about the afterlife... well that is worthwhile too. If there is any money to be made on this, you will certainly receive your fair share. Now, you had better get back to your husband and kids. I thought your husband was very understanding about this whole ordeal. He didn't seem like such a bad guy to me."

"He's a shitwad." Cindy responded. "He's just putting on a good face for your benefit."

"Well, be that as it may. You had better attend to your children. If you feel in danger with your husband, you just let me know and I will be more than happy to help you" my mother offered. I prayed that help did not involve the use of her pistol.

"He's just a dick. I'm in no danger. Believe you me. If he ever touched me or the kids, I would break his neck faster than a Thanksgiving turkey. That spaz couldn't hurt my grandmother." Cindy responded.

"Goodbye Cindy," my mother responded as she abruptly ended the call. She turned to my seemingly comatose sister-in-law. "Janet, are you all right? You look a little green in the gills."

Janet broke her silence and in a soft hesitating voice proclaimed, "Oh, yes. I think so. But with all due respect to you and Della, this is too much for me. I'm going home to Daniel and Jason. If you ever hear me talking about going to a psychic again, just shoot me." Janet stopped herself and eyed my mother cautiously. "Well, not literally. You know what I mean."

My mother smiled and patted her pocketbook. "Don't worry Janet, my little friend is only for rapists and madmen. You're safe!"

Janet covered her mouth and stared silently out the passenger window. I am quite sure she anticipated their relationship would never be the same.

Twenty Two

My mother had vacated her hotel room and now apparently planned on staying in my town house for the indeterminate future. She had made herself quite at home and appeared to be there for the long haul. In the short time she had been there, she had already started to redecorate. She held me and stood motionless in the living room for a time as she looked around. I noticed a new lamp, new curtains, a silhouette-like painting of a woman in a yoga pose and a large glass statue of what appeared to be a man and a woman kneeling before an enormous moon which now occupied center stage on the coffee table.

She placed me temporarily on the chair, touched the strange glass statue, sighed and then proceeded to call her husband Kellin back in Florida on her cell phone. I could only hear one side of the conversation but it did not appear to be their usual banter which, more often than not consisted of an endless exchange of "I love you" and "No, I love you more." This conversation consisted mainly of my mother cycling between three phrases delivered in a sarcastic and seemingly hostile tone. These phrases were "Oh, really?", "Fine!" and "It doesn't matter anymore."

The call ended with my mother shouting into the phone "I will when I am good and goddamn ready. Goodbye Kellin!" Certainly, this was a big departure from their usual lovey-dovey exchanges. I had seldom seen my mother angry and had never seen Kellin express anger either. Obviously, there was trouble in paradise. My mother stared at the cell phone in the palm of her hand for a moment, placed one of her hands on the statue and looked up towards the sky while muttering something incomprehensible to herself.

She sighed once and then produced a marijuana cigarette from what appeared to be a hidden compartment in her brassiere and proceeded to smoke the entire joint without moving from that spot, catching the falling ashes in her palm. When she was done with her smoking, she retrieved me from the chair she had deposited me in and retreated to my bedroom. She then cautiously placed me on a shelf above the bed and stared at me for a few more minutes.

Meanwhile, I was increasingly resenting being trapped in the body of a doll and starting to have unhealthy homicidal thoughts about my innocent Strawberry

Dumpling. I knew she was an unwitting pawn in this ridiculous situation but still, I could not help but thinking that maybe if her head was pulled off or possibly liberated with my mother's pistol, I could return to the now seemingly normal energy ball post-death existence. In addition, staring at my stoned red-eyed elderly mother also made me increasingly uncomfortable.

As I sat for what seemed like an eternity on the shelf in my former bedroom, my mother finally ceased her endless staring and began to pack up my bedroom belongings into cardboard boxes while softly humming to herself. Once in a while, an article would cause her to laugh and more often than not, holding certain things would cause her to cry. As she handled many of the objects, she would talk out loud and recall memories of our times together. After a time, she exited the bedroom but left the bedside lamp illuminated, sparing me from complete darkness. Since I was confined to the bedroom, I could not see where she slept, so I am assuming it was on the couch as my bed remained just as I had left it the morning of my demise.

My only company was two other stuffed animals that were proudly displayed on the shelf along with my own sweet pink persona. She had not packed any of those up just yet. One might have thought this was the bedroom of a fourteen year old girl instead of that of a forty-two year old woman. In reality, only one of my stuffed neighbors, Bo the Bunny, was from childhood. It was a present from my now deceased Nana. The other was a gift I had received as a joke from Penny on my fortieth birthday. It was a stuffed dog with glasses and a cane who bellowed loudly when you pressed his paw "I am Soooooooooooooo Oooooooooooooold! Soooooooooooooo Oooooooooooooold!" It was supposed to be an imitation of a dog's howl but sounded more like a wounded senior citizen who had fallen and couldn't get up.

During one of these endless times of silence and introspection, I did manage to reestablish communication with the Pink Ladies. The one with the strongest presence was Martin, although I also did manage to make a connection with Daphne. Daphne's messages always were of a serious note with recommendations on how to get out of my situation. Although she had never encountered anything like this before, she said more than likely the only way I could escape was to engage in another psychic session and force myself out of the doll's body at that time. In the interim, she recommended concentrating continually and visualizing myself physically exiting the doll's body. I concentrated as hard as I could but still remained hopelessly trapped.

Martin on the other hand, thought this was the best thing since sliced bread. He said he would trade places with me without hesitation if he could get a chance to see the human realm once again. He emphatically stressed that if he had a preference, he would rather possess the body of something a little classier and less frumpy than Strawberry Dumpling. If he had his choice, he said he would choose GI Joe or Barbie since he would prefer to come back with a hot body, regardless of gender. However, he would be satisfied with Strawberry Dumpling and stressed "Girl, I can make even a doll who looks like a hot mess work."

I waited on that shelf for what seemed like forever. Then one day, my mother picked me up and announced that we were headed out on an adventure. As it turned out, it was an adventure which would have a huge impact on my new future. This time my mother did not pack me into her pocketbook which permitted me to have a full view of our journey. We took a taxi from my townhouse to Bradley International Airport and were soon on our way to New York City.

It was a miracle that we ever got on the plane as my mother initially refused to surrender the pistol she kept in her pocketbook. After arguing with the agents at the baggage scan terminal, she was escorted to a special room to be searched. After chastising the female officer for having the gall to frisk a seventy-one year old woman, she succeeded in convincing that officer that she was not planning on hijacking the aircraft and was bringing the pistol with her due to the "high incidences of rape and assault in the city of New York." Eventually, they relented and allowed her to bring the pistol as long as it was emptied of ammunition and as long as she included it in her checked luggage. We missed the first flight, but luckily, there was abundance of flights between Hartford and New York City.

During the airplane ride, my mother actually propped me up in the seat beside her as if I was an actual person. I am guessing she was just lucky enough to have an empty seat beside her as I can't imagine my mother actually paid for a seat for a Strawberry Dumpling doll. All during the flight my mother talked to me like I was actually physically seated in the seat next to her. "I don't know if you can hear me Della," she began, "But just in case let me fill you in."

I learned from our one-sided conversation that we were headed to New York City and were going to be guests on a talk show. I was a little familiar with the show which was called "Kindred Spirits." It featured the colorful and renowned psychic Rosa Lee who was a media darling and was known as the "Movie Star Medium." She was allegedly the psychic confidante of a number of well-known celebrities and at least one ex-President.

I also learned during the flight that people will treat you like you are a little soft in the head if you board a flight with a doll in the next seat over, and talk to it during the entire flight. My mother had seated me in the middle seat and she had taken the aisle due to her frequent need to use the bathroom.

The passenger in the window seat was a Goth-like twenty-something who rolled her eyes incessantly whenever my mother started talking to me. Eventually she put in her earbuds to block out the ramblings of the crazy woman in the aisle seat. However, truth be known, on one of my mother's excursions to the rest room when I was left unattended and vulnerable, the Goth woman did investigate her silent doll neighbor. She removed her earbuds and peered very close at my face for a few uncomfortable minutes as if she expected me to speak. By the time my mother returned though, the Goth woman had resumed her position leaning against the window with her music blaring and giving off a "Get me the hell off this plane" vibe.

The flight attendant had no idea how to handle the situation so she started referring to my mother as "honey" and to the doll beside her as "her little friend."

When the flight attendant offered my mother coffee, she said "Can I get anything for your little friend honey? Maybe she would like some juice or cookies?"

My mother responded, "I don't think so. You do know it is a doll don't you?" The flight attendant looked perplexed, quietly placed the coffee on my mother's tray and did her best to avoid my mother for the remainder of the flight.

My mother, not knowing that a spirit actually inhabited the doll, continued to talk incessantly to me, begging me to do my best to perform something extraordinary on the television show. She also confirmed that if anyone could set my sprit free, it would be Rosa Lee. She also told me that Psychic Suzie, whose name I now learned was Elizabeth LeGare, would also be joining us. Penny and Janet had both declined to take part in the show. Penny did not want to appear on television. Janet, still sufficiently disturbed from her experiences with Hank's doll emporium, continued to distance herself from all things psychic. Cindy, due to her problems with the law, was not allowed out of the state of Massachusetts for the time being. My mother also assured me she had left my little Barry under the care of Penny until "things cleared up" and she could figure out what to do with him. In reality, I felt much more confident with Penny caring for Barry. My mother had a tendency to forget little things involved in the care of a dog like feeding him, giving him water and letting him out to go to the bathroom.

The plane landed and we disembarked without incident. The flight attendant offered a nervous smile as we exited the aircraft. As we passed her, my mother raised my little doll arm, waved it and said loudly "Now say bye bye to the pretty plane lady! " The flight attendant looked mortified and pressed herself against the wall as we exited. My mother said mostly to herself, in her low gravelly voice, "Who says being a senior citizen isn't fun?" She giggled endlessly as we made our way to baggage claim.

"Oooh, this is very exciting!" exclaimed my mother as she dropped me down in the back seat of a waiting taxi and gave the driver the address to the studio. Unlike the flight attendant, the cab driver seemed completely unfazed by the elderly woman and her conversations with her doll. I guessed that with his being a taxi driver in New York City, this may not have been the first time he encountered this situation

Twenty Three

Upon arrival at the studio, we were ushered into what the TV folks refer to as the "green room" or the space where you wait before you take the stage. In reality, the room was not green at all but was colored a sickening shade of pink.

Despite the success of the program, the room was a little bit worse for the wear. The pink paint was flaking off the walls in various places and I could not help but be reminded of the calamine lotion my mother used to spread liberally on me during my frequent bouts of poison ivy. The lotion dried up into pink scabs that would flake off in a most disgusting manner. Often forced to go to school with way too much lotion applied, I often felt like a Mary Kay leper.

The rest of the room was decorated with couches and upholstered chairs in an assortment of other bright colors which made the room look even more garish. Although Rosa Lee may have been a talented psychic and TV personality, if she was responsible for this room, her interior decorating skills left much to be desired.

Soon after we arrived, we were joined by Psychic Suzie. As I mentioned, I had since learned her name was actually Elizabeth LeGare but I have continued to refer to her as Psychic Suzie since that is the name I had become accustomed to. Suzie seemed to be in quite a tizzy and was a whirlwind of activity as she tried to converse with my mother. In between her various sentences, she made a strange puffing sound like she was about to blow out birthday candles on a cake.

"Helen, it is so good to see you..." Suzie began and then puffed three times. "Oh my goodness, we will be on in less than fifteen minutes. My hair is just a wreck. Isn't there a makeup person here? Did they do your hair?" She puffed three times again. "I have never met Rosa Lee. Have you met her? Probably not. I mean I haven't met her..." She emitted four more puffs. My experience prior to this point had painted Suzie as a pretty cool and collected lady but apparently the thought of being on TV with Rosa Lee was a bit more than she could handle. In addition to her puffing, she started to talk very rapidly without interruption. My mother barely had a chance to respond.

"I mean don't they give you a primer or a training session or something. Are we expected just to walk on stage without any preparation? I mean what are they going to want us to say? Will there be cue cards?" She ended her last diatribe with one loud puff.

"Elizabeth," my mother responded. "You need to calm down. Didn't you get the packet the studio sent? It gave us a checklist and the main topics Rosa would be asking us about. Here, I still have a copy."

"Oh, I did read that. I have a copy somewhere. It is in my purse I think. Oh my God, where's my purse? It was here a minute ago. Where's my purse?" She now continued to puff without stopping and started pacing back and forth.

"Elizabeth," my mother said in a soothing tone, "sweetie, your purse is right here on the chair. You need to calm down. The universe will provide you everything you need for this to be a success. Now, come and sit down next to me and just relax. You are a talented woman and have nothing to be worried about."

The door to the green room opened and a young blonde woman entered. She was quite striking and although she was attractive, it was her extremely long fingernails, her eyeshadow and her outfit which really made her stand out. Her fingernails were an overly bright hue of pink and her eyelids were shaded bright blue, festooned with tiny glittering stars. Her baby blue eyes sparkled merrily from underneath the garish eyeshadow. She wore a red faux leather mini-skirt topped with an orange top which was oddly decorated with blue and yellow feathers. I suspected this may have been the woman who decorated the green room. She pulled a small trolley of cosmetics behind her.

"Hello ladies. My name is Starburst. Ms. Lee is so excited to have you on the show. We'll be bringing you on stage in... umm... about ten minutes or so. I just wanted to do a quick make-up check before we headed out there. You both look lovely but the TV cameras can accentuate wrinkles and blemishes and such so we just want to make sure you look good!"

"I think we can skip Ms. Dumpling's makeup," she giggled with a glance towards my limp doll body. She then, in what seemed like a whirlwind of powders, lotions and smells, took action on first my mother and then Psychic Suzie. I watched in amusement as her four plus inch nails did their magic, fully expecting my mother or Suzie to suffer a laceration or two. My mother remained calm through the whole thing although she kept glancing around the room for what I suspect was a mirror to assure that Starburst had not done anything crazy like painted half-moons on her eyelids. Poor Suzie continued to puff through the entire makeover with a couple of, what I can only describe as soft whimpers interspersed with her non-stop puffing. Starburst concluded her operation with a sigh and stepped back to admire her quick and efficient work. "You both look perfect!" Starburst's phone buzzed.

"Well girls, it looks like its show time!" Starburst exclaimed. "Follow me and don't be nervous! Just pretend like it's your living room!"

All three exited, but within thirty seconds my mother dashed back and grabbed my Dumpling body abruptly by the arm. "Oh, Dumpling!" She exclaimed. "I almost forgot you... and you're really the star of the show!" She emphasized the point with a big raspy laugh. Suzie and my mother, with me in tow, stepped onto the stage.

Rosa Lee greeted us with a big smile and first hugged Suzie and then my mother. I felt a little left out as neither Strawberry Dumpling nor I was acknowledged. I had obviously not seen Rosa Lee before in person but she seemed to emanate beauty, confidence and charisma from every cell in her body. It was difficult to tell her ethnicity but her light brown skin glowed with health and vigor. Her luxurious shoulder length dark brown hair only added to her allure and beauty. Although they could have been contacts, her eyes glowed the most

151

beautiful shade of emerald green which was expertly accentuated by taupe eye shadow. Her lips were painted a subdued shade of red which added to her glamour without being tacky. If I had been into women and if Rosa was into Strawberry Dumpling dolls, I may have asked her out on a date.

"It is so wonderful to see you ladies. Welcome to the show!" Her voice unlike the rest of her perfectly coiffed image did have a slightly annoying gravelly quality to it. At least God has chosen to give her one weakness, I thought. Life could be so unfair when divvying out looks.

"Pardon my voice," she continued, "I am just getting over a cold and sound a little rough."

"Perfect. There goes my theory about God being fair." I thought.

"I am familiar with your story and have watched the video at least eighty times. So intriguing! So exciting!" Rosa exclaimed. "Mrs. Hampton, if I could have you sit in this seat here right beside me…"

"Please call me Helen," my mother interrupted. "I think 'Mrs.' is so limiting and I have remarried since Della's father died, although I kept Hampton as my last name."

"Oh, of course, Helen. Please forgive me. If you could sit here Helen…" Rosa instructed, gesturing towards the chair, "and if you could place the doll in the chair just to your right." My mother sat and placed me in the chair beside her as instructed.

"And Elizabeth. I cannot tell you how excited I am to meet you. Your reputation in the psychic community precedes you and we are so happy you could make it. If you could take this chair…" she motioned for Elizabeth to be seated in the other empty chair.

"Thank you so much." Psychic Suzie responded. The compliment had seemed to calm her somewhat as her puffing appeared to now be on the decline. "You have no idea how happy I am to meet you and be on the show!"

"The same goes for me." Rosa replied. "We're just about to return from the commercial break. Just try to be relaxed. I know live TV can be nerve-wracking. Let's just pretend we're just a bunch of girlfriends having a chat over coffee, OK? Try to ignore the studio audience. We won't be taking questions so just pretend they're not there if that helps."

Although I could not see her from my vantage point, I surmised that Psychic Suzie had not previously realized there was an audience. The live audience was somewhat obscured by the stage lights. However, judging by the new series of puffs coming from my right, I thought Rosa's instructions had definitely not helped with Suzie's nerves.

A voice from behind us proclaimed. "OK everyone...we're on in 5... 4... 3... 2... 1"

Twenty Four

"Welcome back everyone!" Rosa announced to the camera. "I am sure many of you who are interested in psychic phenomena have now seen the famous Internet video of the Dancing Doll. I have watched it many times myself, and have found it extremely interesting. I understand the video has surpassed the five million viewer mark within just the first week of it being posted. It has intrigued those of us in the psychic community, but it has also been criticized by many as being a fabrication amid allegations that the video is fake or was manipulated in some way. We are so very fortunate to have with us two women who appeared in this video and can help us to judge its validity as well as the reality of the psychic session that was filmed. And... we also have the actual doll here today too!" The audience clapped and shouted their approval. Clearly, it was impossible for my mother and Suzie to ignore the audience now.

"First, I'd like to introduce Helen Hampton. Helen is the mother of Della Hampton, whose spirit allegedly took possession of the doll you see seated next to her. Welcome to the program, Helen."

"Thank you so much. I am very pleased to be here. And there's no 'alleged' about it," my mother warned. "That doll was definitely possessed by my daughter's spirit."

"I am sure that is true and the audience is excited to hear all about it. So happy to have you here Helen! Please accept my condolences on the loss of your daughter." Rosa responded. The audience clapped once again.

"We are also fortunate to have with us a rising star in the Psychic community. Elizabeth Legare is also with us today. Elizabeth is the medium who conducted the séance which is featured in the video. A very warm welcome to you too Elizabeth!"

"Thank you very much. It is an honor and a privilege to be here today." began Psychic Suzie. There was then an uncomfortable pause punctuated by three puffs. "I must admit I am a little nervous though. I have never been on television before."

"Well... you are surrounded by supporters and admirers. Am I right audience?" Rosa replied as she extended her hand to the audience.

The audience exploded with approval and from what I could gather from my vantage point, Psychic Suzie seemed to relax a little once more.

"Before we begin our conversation which I cannot WAIT to discuss, can we see the video clip which has captured the nation's interest?" Rosa asked of her unseen crew.

The video played on a big screen above our heads. Although I could not see it, I could hear everyone's recorded voices. Cindy had not captured the whole event but had evidently filmed the doll dancing, the doll crashing to the table top and finished with the lights going out. Cindy's voice stood out as we heard her say, "Can we give her a knife and have her stab my friggin' dirt bag of a husband? Not too kill him... just to (bleep) freak him out. Holy crap!" The audience exploded in laughter. I wondered how the viral video clip had helped Cindy's domestic situation. I also wasn't sure if sharing the fact that you wanted to have a doll stab your husband would register as a criminal offense. However, it sounded like Cindy was in enough hot water with the criminal justice system as it was.

"Well... that was quite the event! " Rosa exclaimed, doing her best to control her laughter. Now, there were three other women in that video. "Can you tell us who they are?"

"Yes," my mother responded. "My daughter-in-law Janet; Penny, a friend of my daughters; and the one who wanted the doll to kill her husband... well that is an old college friend, Cindy, that my daughter used to work with. I promise you she is quite a colorful character! She is unavailable to be here today... due to circumstances I am not at liberty to discuss." My mother concluded her statement with a cute giggle and covered her mouth with her hand. This set the audience on fire. My mother amazed me! For a woman who barely spoke my entire childhood, she seemed right at home on the talk show circuit!

"You are just as cute as you can be Helen." Rosa responded. "Audience, don't you think Helen is a cutie?"

The audience voiced its approval with thunderous applause.

"Helen, as I understand, after your daughter's death, you and your daughter-in-law employed the services of Ms. Legare to make contact with your daughter. Was the recorded session the first session where you made contact?"

"No. No." my mother assured her. "It was the second session. My daughter-in-law and Elizabeth made initial contact with her during the first session. It just wasn't until the second session that we saw Little Miss Strawberry Dumpling here strut her stuff." Again, my mother suppressed a giggle and the audience responded its approval. My mother was starting to get caught up in the celebrity of the situation.

"If I may," began Psychic Suzie, "we had conducted several sessions, and in each one, Della's spirit was strong. I asked Helen to bring something to the last two sessions that would have a strong connection to her daughter. The doll was something that held great meaning to her." A few little puffs followed her explanation although they were definitely becoming few and far between once again.

"I have seldom seen such a strong presence," continued Psychic Suzie. "It was just as if Della was in the room with us. We attempted to connect during our last session but could get no response although I felt her energy was still very strong. As a matter of fact, I can feel her energy here today."

"May I hold the doll?" Rosa inquired.

"Certainly," My mother responded. "But be careful. You never know when she will want to do the hokie pokie!" The audience once again voiced its approval. Clearly my mother was taking advantage of her five minutes of fame.

Rosa held the doll and closed her eyes. "Mmmm-hmmm, mmmm-hmmm" Rosa affirmed. "I can definitely feel something myself. Girlfriend, the energy doesn't lie."

Although difficult to describe, I felt an intense pressure. I am not sure if it was pressure on the body of the doll which I inhabited or something else. However, it was an almost unbearable pressure and it somehow seemed to draw me with an uncontrollable force towards Rosa Lee.

Although I cannot be certain exactly what happened next, my vision took on a kaleidoscope quality. Fractured images of the audience, my mother, Psychic Suzie and others floated in and out of my field of vision. The next thing I knew there were screams, lights flashed and the smell of smoke filled the air, and then pandemonium seemed to take hold. The only thing that seemed constant was the face of Rosa Lee in the middle of my field of vision. I heard the *pop* sound that I now realized was a harbinger of things to come. I then saw Rosa's eyes widen, her lips part and then I heard her voice say in a seemingly calm tone. "Oh Lord!"

Twenty Five

Everything appeared to be in chaos after this episode and it took me a little bit to figure out what exactly had happened. One thing was clear though. I was no longer confined to the body of Strawberry Dumpling. I was now able to see everything seemingly at once and was no longer confined by the vision range of the doll.

Although it is impossible to describe in words, the closest description is that I was sort of *floating*, high above the chaos below. It was as if I could see the whole studio at once but could at the same time see the individual events occurring as if I was right next to them. I also now seemed to be able to hear various conversations at the same time, but was somehow able to distinguish what was being said in each conversation, although they occurred simultaneously. It was pretty damn cool. I felt like a Superhero, maybe Wonder Woman without the cool outfit and the awesome beach body.

One of the first things I noticed was that Rosa Lee was on the ground, kind of half sitting up. She was holding her head and had a kind of crazy half smile on her face. She looked like she had gotten drunk and fallen down, but was now ready to get back up and rejoin the party. What was left of the Strawberry Dumpling doll lay beside her. Apparently, the doll had caught fire because it lay smoking on the ground just to her right. Rosa's assistant Starburst, was kneeling beside her assuring her that we were off the air.

"I certainly hope they got that on film. The ratings are going to skyrocket after this." Rosa overemphasized the word "Sky" so it sound more like "Skyyyyyyyy."

"We got it on film" Starburst assured her. "The WEB site and our Facebook page are already exploding and it is being tweeted all over the place."

"Fantastic!" responded Rosa. "That was just unbelievable! The doll just exploded and I swear I saw a spirit cloud pop right out of there. I hope that shows up on film."

"We've already checked it and everything is there." Starburst further assured her.

"How is my face?" Rosa inquired. "Did I get burned? I hope this wig is alright. This thing cost me a fortune."

"You look great. Just a little sprucing up and you'll be as good as new."

"Perfect," said Rosa, her face now smiling broadly. "We need to get back to my office and figure out what we are going to do next. This is going to shoot our ratings through the roof! I have never experienced anything like that before. I mean, of course, I have never experienced anything like that on camera."

Rosa tentatively stood up and brushed at her hair with her hands. She then placed both hands on top of her head and made an adjustment to what I now knew was a wig. She glanced around the studio as if she was assessing the damage. The wide grin never left her face. "Starburst, get Mr. Dempsey on the phone. Tell him it's urgent! We need to talk immediately! Also, make sure our guests here are taken care of." She pointed towards my mother and Psychic Suzie.

"Right away, Ms. Lee," Starburst responded. "I'm on it."

Rosa looked down at her hands and held them out in front of her as if seeing them for the first time, then placed them on each side of her face. "Thank you baby Jesus!" she announced loudly and then stood up.

Meanwhile the audience was still trying to figure out what happened. Several people had fainted and a sizable crowd was forcing their way to the door while security officers tried to maintain some level of control. About ten or twelve other audience members were trying to get as close to the stage as possible and taking pictures and videos with their cell phones. One security guard was doing his best to hold up his hands and shield the stage from them, while yelling "Stop It! Please exit through the doors in back for the safety of everyone! Come on folks! Get out of here!"

My mother remained in her seat seemingly as cool as a cucumber and looked to be awaiting further instructions. "Is the show over?" she repeatedly inquired to no one in particular. "Are we still on the air?" Getting no response she quietly sipped her glass of water and watched everything going on with what seemed a subdued amusement.

Psychic Suzie looked a little traumatized and was now puffing so much, she sounded like a little diesel train struggling to make it up a hill. She also held tightly on to the arms of her chair with both hands as if she expected it to become airborne along with her at any moment. "This isn't good," she muttered, and emphasized the point with no less than seven puffs. "This is definitely not good. " She then kept turning her head from side to side as she muttered repeatedly. "Not good." Puff! Puff! Puff! "Not good." Puff! Puff! Puff! I fully expected her to start slapping herself at any moment, at which point the orderlies would show up to put her in a straitjacket and send her off to the loony bin...err...psychiatric institution. One should at least try to be politically correct, even in death.

Twenty Six

Well, as I said, I was experiencing something peculiar and hard to describe. I was floating above the foray but also felt somehow like I was everywhere else in the immediate vicinity at the same time. After steadying herself, and with help from her assistant Starburst, Rosa Lee had bid a quick goodbye to my mother and the muttering Psychic Suzie and both she and Starburst quickly exited the main stage.

Once Rosa had departed, my mother stood up quietly, brushed off her skirt, crossed the stage and retrieved the smoldering Strawberry Dumpling. "Oh my dear," my mother said to the doll, "I am not sure if you are still in there, but it looks like this doll has seen better days." She gazed at the doll for a few moments and then placed it in a sitting position in Rosa's chair. She then looked around the studio, eventually gazing up towards the ceiling and said quietly, "I hope you are at peace my little girl. Certainly, this fiasco was not peaceful. We'll see what we can do."

She then turned to Psychic Suzie and said "My dear, are you alright? Perhaps, we should get you an inhaler? What do you think we should do now? Should we do another séance to see if we can contact my daughter?"

Psychic Suzie puffed three times and turned towards my mother. "Frankly Helen, this has been a little too much for me. " She puffed about six more times in sequence. "I think I may need to take a break from the psychic business for a little while. I can feel Della's presence here today though. I feel like she is definitely watching over us."

Suddenly, Rosa Lee appeared on the stage again. "Ladies, the network has just asked me if I would be willing to host a half hour psychic special where we would attempt to contact Della. Our episode today has created quite the media frenzy and I don't think I could do it without your help. People are dying to learn more about the afterlife and this was an extremely rare and exciting occurrence captured on film."

"Oh I don't know..." began my mother. "I am not sure I want to pursue this any further. I only started this because I wanted to make sure that Della was able to move on... to gain some peace in the afterlife."

Psychic Suzie stated "I was just telling Helen, this ordeal has been a little too much for me. I am thinking of taking a respite from the psychic world, at least for a while. I don't think I would really be up for another show."

"I wish you would reconsider," Rosa responded. "The network is willing to pay each of you thirty thousand dollars for your appearance. Of course, all your meals and lodging will be covered too. I wish you'd reconsider!"

"I could definitely be up for it for thirty thousand dollars!" exclaimed Psychic Suzie. "I am sure a warm bath and a bottle of Pinot can calm my nerves." Apparently, the good old American dollar and not an inhaler was the prescription she needed.

"Splendid!" Rosa responded. "It will be great and your career is going to skyrocket. I'll have Starburst send you a case of Pinot!" Mrs. Hampton... errr... Helen... can we convince you to join us?"

"Well..." My mother responded tentatively "On a few conditions."

"Anything" Rosa responded. "What would make you change your mind?"

"Thirty <u>five</u> thousand dollars, and I will need a complete New York City makeover. I'll need my hair done. Manicure. Pedicure. A new outfit too. I'll need to have bottled spring water, ginger tea and shortbread cookies available at all times as well." Who was this woman? My mother was becoming quite the prima donna negotiator.

"I am sure we can arrange for all of that!" Rosa Lee answered. "This is fantastic! They have asked us to start filming in three days. You may as well stay in the city! I'll have Starburst arrange everything! This is going to be big ladies! "

"What do we do about the doll?" My mother questioned. "I don't think it is going to be as useful to us now. Not to mention, it is not exactly photogenic in its current state."

"We will need something that is meaningful to Della if we want to make a connection again," Psychic Suzie warned. "Is there something other than the doll that Della felt especially close to, Helen?"

"Well there is always Barry, her dog. She loved him more than anything else. Can we use a live animal to make a connection?"

"We can make it work" responded Psychic Suzie.

"We can have the dog and the doll." Rosa Lee confirmed. "We'll have the doll on set for people to see as I am sure we will be interspersing the clip from today's show. The doll will be a visual reminder of the powerful connection we previously made."

"Della," Rosa Lee said loudly speaking out into the now empty audience seating area. "If you are still here… we are so thankful for your help! Thank you so much for joining us! You are going to show everyone that there is an afterlife… that the psychic world is real… you may just change the way people view the world as we know it! Thank you! Thank you!"

Despite her obvious hunger for celebrity, Rosa Lee did seem sincere and I must admit I did feel a little excited! "If the Pink Ladies could see me now!" I thought. Excitement welled up in me. I never really felt like I had been noticed that much in life. Now, in death, I was about to not just get my fifteen minutes of fame but maybe even a half-hour! My mother, Rosa Lee and Psychic Suzie could ride on my coattails. Selfishly or not, I intended for this to be the Della show. Was this too egotistical? Was I breaking some cosmic rule? Was I even going to be able to make anything happen on the show? I wasn't sure. But whether this was bad or good, I was really, really excited! I felt like I was going to explode!

I once again heard the now infamous popping sound and before I knew what was happening, the sprinkler system went off in the studio and it started spraying water all over the stage, seats and camera equipment. Staff members appeared seemingly out of nowhere moving equipment and seeking to stop the flow of water.

"Well!" Rosa Lee exclaimed. "I think we have our answer from Della."

"Come with me ladies" Rosa Lee said as she guided them towards the door. "Let's get the ball rolling."

I watched them exit and amused myself with watching the staff scramble to control the water damage. I must admit I was starting to feel quite powerful again, although I did feel a little bad for the staff. Perhaps, I could create a windstorm in the studio to help them with the cleanup? As I pondered what psychic tricks I might be able to concoct next, I could feel the strong psychic pull of Daphne and Martin trying to get my attention. I attempted to focus. I did miss my Pink Ladies and was eager to let them know what was happening to me now!

Twenty Seven

I was finding it easier and easier now to communicate with Daphne and Martin and they told me it was getting easier and easier for them to connect with me as well. Although Daphne was a little concerned and cautious about my newfound psychic celebrity, Martin was perhaps more excited than me.

"Girl, I would love to be on a TV show! You are so lucky!" Martin told me excitedly.

"It is kind of exciting." Daphne agreed. "It is a chance to let the whole world know that there is something beyond death, even if we still don't know what it all means."

"Why don't you guys join me?" I communicated. "Maybe with a little practice we can get you to make a connection too. Right now, I feel completely free. It's hard to explain the feeling but it is fantastic. At the very least, we could probably set up some communication between you and your family… even if I had to relay your messages."

"Oh I don't know," began Daphne, "I tried that before with my husband and it was very emotionally draining. I am not even sure how long it has been. He has probably moved on. No need to open up old wounds."

"Della, I am all for opening up old wounds!" Martin said excitedly. "I never really got to say goodbye to Jose. I would love the chance to do that and to find out what has happened to him since I died."

"Well, let me see what we can do!" I responded. "We have some time before the show. We can at least experiment and see what is possible. It is worth a shot."

"It can't hurt to try it," Daphne finally agreed. "Besides, it is doing the world a service, if we can let them know that they need not be so afraid of death."

"We'll need to really beef up our energy reserves though," Daphne added, "We know that weird things can happen if we do not have enough energy."

"Weird things have worked out very well for Della!" Martin responded excitedly. "I am all for weird things. I mean, what can really happen to us? We're already dead!"

"That's true." Daphne agreed. "And frankly Della, it's been a little boring around here without you. Let's give it a shot! The girls have been asking about you. They really miss you! I have been keeping them informed of your escapades. I really think they are living vicariously through you."

"Living? Daphne, you do know us Pink Ladies are dead, right? But I am sure they are <u>dying</u> to hear the latest," Martin joked.

"Ha! Ha! Very funny, Martin. It was just a figure of speech. Besides, Della is living in a sense. She is at least partially part of the living world."

"True, true." Martin agreed. "Della, you are a trailblazer. You are bringing the pizazz back to death. You might just get your own television series, girl. And please be advised that if you do, yours truly should be one of your first guests. I can see it now. You could call your show 'Dead Della Dishes Dirt.' I can be one of your field reporters from the great beyond."

"Let's not get ahead of ourselves, Martin," I forewarned him. "But I do like the sound of that. Dead Della Dishes Dirt! It has a nice ring. However, one step at a time. I can't be setting dolls on fire and setting off sprinklers every time I want to make a connection."

"Della, people eat that stuff right up!" Martin responded. "You could be ushering in a whole new era for the dead. And don't forget us little people when you gain fame and glory."

"Martin," I assured him, "There is no way I could ever forget you. So don't worry about that."

"Truer words have never been spoken," Daphne agreed. "Well Della, you are the expert now so just let us know what we can do or how we can help. We're ready, willing and able."

"And fabulous," Martin added, "Ready, willing, able and fabulous!"

"And fabulous," I concurred. "We are definitely that!"

Twenty Eight

I remained in the studio awaiting further contact from either Rosa Lee and/or Psychic Suzie and was amazed at the amount of activities that occurred here at all hours of the day and night. I had never been on a television set before and had assumed that Rosa Lee's studio was used only for her show. However, this studio was transformed a number of times during the day and night for the filming of various other TV shows.

A morning talk show, a local newscast, a situational comedy episode, as well as Rosa Lee's normal daily show were filmed in the same studio. The crew magically and quickly transformed the stage for each filming as well as removing all evidence that the studio had earlier been the subject of a sprinkler system spray down and the now infamous Strawberry Dumpling explosion.

Martin, Daphne and I continued to communicate almost without interruption while we waited for the show taping to begin. As part of our communication, we also experimented with what physical feats we might be able to perform in anticipation of the television special. It proved impossible for Daphne and Martin to accomplish anything on their own since they were unable to visually see the studio, and basically needed me as a conduit for communication. However, I was becoming a champ at making things happen in the physical world to the surprise and astonishment of the studio personnel, actors, newscasters and audience members, who filtered in an out of the studio in what seemed like an endless parade. The three of us, however, experienced no shortage of amusement although Daphne and Martin had to be content with my descriptions of what was happening. With Daphne and Martin concentrating with me on the task at hand, my abilities seemed to know no bounds.

During the broadcast of one of the local newscasts, I found that with concentration, I could take control of the cameras as long as I was aware of which camera was the active camera, which proved difficult at points. The morning newscast featured an overly handsome and overly pompous news anchor named John Coxwell who seemed to be constantly demeaning his female co-anchor and production staff at breaks and whenever they were off-air.

You would surmise that the two news anchors were the best of friends when you saw them on the air, but as soon as the director announced that they were temporarily off-air, Coxwell proceeded to comment relentlessly on his co-anchor's choice of clothes and the ineptitude of much of the staff.

When the camera was not focused on him, he would roll his eyes, make faces and sarcastically mimic the words of his co-anchor or the reporters clearly illustrating that he thought everyone but himself was completely without talent. He also insisted that everyone refer to him as Mr. Coxwell and not as John. How this jerk managed to keep his position was beyond me.

When the camera shifted to his co-anchor, I was able to force the camera back to him so that the TV audience could see his juvenile antics. The camera crew quickly switched cameras when this happened, but not before the TV audience got a glimpse of what an ass this guy was. I was able to make this happen three separate times before the jerk was cognizant that his ridiculous antics were being transmitted to the masses. His lovely co-anchor did her best to retain her cool throughout the incident, and had obviously learned to tune him out long ago. She, however, could not stop a slight smile escaping from her lips once she realized what was happening, despite the tragic news she was reporting on.

Once the newscast was complete, Mr. Coxwell exploded with a series of expletives aimed primarily at the head camera technician telling him that he was inept and could easily be replaced and that he could expect to lose his job over this. The cameraman, who obviously had been pushed past his breaking point, responded "Listen Mr. Cox-Swell..." with an intentional and emphatic pause between the syllables. "I'm not sure what happened. The camera seemed to have a mind of its own, but I am so glad that your ridiculous juvenile-shit behavior got on air, and I wouldn't be surprised if you end up being the one out of a job. I have been here fourteen years and I am Union... so you can take your little wimp sniveling ass right up to the big boss... and see what happens... you little prick!"

Mr. Coxwell's co-anchor could not contain herself any longer and burst into uncontrollable laughter and was soon joined by most of the camera crew and production staff. Like a little kid, Mr. Coxwell's eyes watered up and he literally stamped his feet and walked out of the studio. The laughter continued for many minutes thereafter.

We also had some fun during the taping of the TV sitcom. From what I gathered, it appeared to be a series of pilot episodes that the studio was pitching in hopes that it would be approved for prime time use. It revolved around two roommates who had moved together from a

179

town in rural Maine to mid-town Manhattan and their experience fitting into the city. It was tentatively titled "Fifth and Maine."

The actors all seemed a likeable enough sort and seemed to all get along very well and respect each other, unlike the environment fostered by the aforementioned Mr. Coxwell. Although there was a small audience present for the taping, it was not filmed live so I felt a little less guilty about my interference with this show. However, I did cause the director to yell "cut" much more than anyone would have liked.

The main characters names were Reggie and Raleigh and one of the catch phrases that appeared numerous times in the show was the Reggie character, as well as the other characters in the show, greeting Raleigh with the catch phrase "What's up dude?" This reminded me of a drinking game we used to play in college called "Hi Bob" where we would all gather around to watch reruns of the Bob Newhart show. Every time someone said "Hi Bob," you were required to take a drink. So I decided that every time the phrase "What's up dude" was spoken, I would have something fly up on the stage from the audience area. I managed to propel a hat, a pocketbook, a cell phone and a pair of sunglasses among a number of other things.

After a half-dozen times, I stopped, as I started feeling a little too evil. The audience was bearing the brunt of the scolding from the director. I felt guilty casting blame on the audience except for one woman with bleach blonde hair and dark sunglasses. I mean what kind of person wears dark sunglasses inside of a lit studio anyway? And just in case it crossed your mind, she was not blind! I was beginning to see how haunting might just be fun and incredibly addictive. I was thinking if this kept up, I might have to attend a few PA meetings. That is Poltergeists Anonymous for those of you still in the human realm. Seriously though, other than a few other minor events, the rest of our ephemeral performances were much more restrained and only minimally disruptive.

Twenty Nine

Once Rosa Lee arrived, the studio took on a frenetic buzz. You could sense the excitement. There was no audience for the taping and everyone involved seemed a little more relaxed at the prospect. The stage had been transformed from Rosa Lee's normal set to one that resembled more of a Victorian living room, complete with heavily upholstered chairs, a large and ornate couch and a mahogany coffee table, which occupied center stage. Various psychic paraphernalia had been placed about the set including a very ornate set of Tarot Cards, a Ouija board, a crystal ball and an assortment of electronic devices which apparently were used to measure psychic phenomena.

Candles were lit and fragrant incense burned, giving the stage a smoky and mysterious aura. My scorched Strawberry Dumpling doll's body occupied a prominent place at the top of an ornate pedestal that stood beside the couch. The poor little thing looked like she had been recovered from a war zone. Her dress had been almost completely burned and her face was covered in soot and smudges.

Rosa Lee and Starburst appeared first, deeply engrossed in conversation. My mother and Psychic Suzie joined them on stage once Stardust departed. Following them onto the stage was my best friend Penny! What a wonderful surprise! Held securely in Penny's arms was my beautiful little dog Barry. Barry stared off into space and even though I did not know where I physically was, I could not escape the feeling that he was staring right at me.

A myriad of other personnel also joined them on stage and the environs of the studio filled quickly, efficiently, and almost silently with the camera crew and production staff. A light skinned muscular fortyish Hispanic man emerged from the audience area and introduced himself as the Director Manny Rivera. He welcomed everyone and assured them that unlike Rosa's regular show, this was a taped show and it would be filmed in short segments. This seemed to decrease the stress level of my mother and especially Psychic Suzie, who I did not hear puff even once.

Manny then became quite engrossed in conversation with Penny, and although I did not listen to their conversation, Penny's responses were punctuated with girlish giggles. This was unusual for Penny because she is not the kind of woman who would generally be described as "girly", and most assuredly not as "gigglish." As the conversation between the two of them continued, Penny relinquished control of Barry to my mother, and Manny guided Penny off the stage with his hand placed gently in the small of her back. Penny then took a seat in the first row of the audience area. Manny joined the production staff at the rear of the studio.

After taking a half-hour to get everyone fitted with microphones and various rearrangements of items on the stage, the taping began. Rosa Lee recorded an introduction where she reviewed the events that had led up to the special, introduced my mother, Barry and Psychic Suzie and explained that the purpose of the special was to attempt to connect with the afterworld. She emphasized that both my mother and Psychic Suze were not actors and referred to clips of both the Kindred Spirits episode, where I had apparently exploded out of the doll as well as the Internet video clip, where I had caused the doll to maniacally dance on the table top.

"Now," began Rosa Lee, "we will attempt to reconnect with this very powerful spirit right here tonight. Expect the unexpected! Since Elizabeth was the first psychic to make contact with Della Hampton, we will have her take the lead, and I will lend my psychic energy as well."

"Let's all join hands," Psychic Suzie (aka. Elizabeth) advised "and let us all picture Della in our mind's eye and see if we can bring her forward." Suzie then lit a candle in the center of the table and they all joined hands. The studio's lights dimmed.

"Della..." Suzie began. "If you can hear us, please give us a sign. Your mother is here as well as your beloved dog Barry. Can you send us a signal to let us know you can hear us?"

I glanced around the studio, somehow being able to see everyone clearly despite the dimness. The camera crew, the production staff, Manny, and Penny were all fixated on the glowing candle. I hesitated. I did not want to start out too big as I wanted to build momentum and show increasingly dramatic phenomena. I made sure I had a connection with both Daphne and Martin and asked them what our first trick of the day should be.

"How about something subdued like making the candle flame grow bigger and smaller to build up a sense of anticipation?" Daphne offered.

"How about we make the candle explode?" Martin suggested with an evil little giggle.

We settled on something in between and I caused the candle to move around in ever larger circles on the tabletop. It was nothing too extreme, but seemed to meet the expectations of everyone involved.

"Thank you Della," Psychic Suzie said. "Now... if it is OK with you, we would like to see if you can provide us any direct communication to allow you to convey any messages you may have."

Suzie placed the Ouija board on the table. I always disliked Ouija boards because every time I used one in my youth, my friends would cause it to spell a silly message that they had apparently discussed beforehand like "Della Loves David Downey" or "Della has smelly feet." Before anyone could place their fingers on the pointer, I assumed control and had it randomly circle the board. This was the spirit equivalent of "I'm thinking" as I was not sure yet what I would say. I kept Martin and Daphne updated on what was happening.

Martin offered "Have it say 'Please call Jose at (206) 231-3789 and tell him it's Martin on the line. Just kidding. This is your show, pudding!"

I could not come up with anything fantastically original so I simply spelled out "HI MOM. I'M FINE. HOW ARE YOU?"

"Oh Sweet Jesus!" my mother responded. "My little girl! I miss you so much! Barry is here and misses you too! I am so sorry about your doll." Suzie and Rosa Lee were beaming from ear to ear. I was quite sure this was going to catapult their careers into super orbit.

I spelled back. "I MISS YOU TOO MOM. DON'T WORRY ABOUT THE DOLL. MY FAULT. LOL"

"What is LOL?" my mother asked.

"Laugh out Loud," Rosa Lee responded with a chuckle.

I wished someone had given me a rulebook. I am pretty sure you were not supposed to treat the Ouija board like some supernatural texting device.

"Are you at peace?" Suzie asked. "Is there anything we can do to help you to the other side?"

I spelled back. "NOPE. I AM OK."

Rosa Lee then asked "Della. Thank you so much for joining us. Can you tell us and the viewers at home what it is like on the other side?"

I responded back "ITS NOT TOO BAD. KIND OF BORING. NOT IN HEAVN YET." There was no apostrophe available on the Ouija board and I cringed a bit as I knew the use of "Its" without the apostrophe was grammatically incorrect. I also somehow missed the second E in Heaven. This was a total oversight as I totally know how to spell 'Heaven.' It is too bad Ouija boards don't have AutoCorrect.

Rosa Lee continued to take over the questioning and Psychic Suzie was starting to appear a little perturbed at the change of control. "Are you alone Della? Are there others with you? Have you had contact with others that have passed on?"

I responded. "WITH NEW FRIENDS MARTIN AND DAPHNE. HAVENT SEEN ANYONE I KNOW YET."

As I continued to keep Daphne and Martin informed of the events, Martin said "Girl, this is getting downright boring. What are they going to ask next? What are you wearing?"

In a change from her normal calm demeanor, Daphne agreed. "Yeah. Martin's right. Let's give them something memorable. What use was all that practice, if we're only going to answer Twenty Questions?"

"What happened to you wanting to educate the masses?" Martin responded sarcastically.

"I still want to but something exciting will draw them in further"

I realized at this point I had dazed out as I was listening to Martin and Daphne, and had apparently missed a question that my mother was asking. "Repeat the question Helen," Suzie instructed my mother.

My mother repeated her question. "I asked if there is anything you wanted to tell us. Any unfinished business?"

"TELL CINDY I'M SORRY. TELL PENNY AND BARRY I MISS THEM" I spelled out.

"Jeez" I thought "Being dead is pretty boring. All the things that happened to me and all I can think of to communicate is about as exciting as a bag of beans."

At Martin and Daphne's urging, I decided we needed a little more excitement. I made the table rise in the air and spin a little to the left and the right being as careful as I could not to hit anyone. I then softly returned it back to its original spot. With Martin and Daphne assisting me with their energies, I also made the tarot card deck start to shoot the cards out one-by-one.

"Oh my dear, does she want to play cards?" My mother exclaimed with hands on both sides of her face and her lips forming an "O." She looked like a silent movie star forced to exit a stagecoach that had just been stopped by bandits. The camera zoomed in for a close-up. My mother held the pose and looked directly into the

189

camera. I fully expected her to say, "I'm ready for my close-up Mr. Rivera."

Giving my mother an "I can't believe you" look, Psychic Suzie recouped control of the spotlight and began to provide an explanation to the audience about the incredulousness of what they were observing and the rarity for such events to be captured on camera.

Before she could get very far though from out of nowhere a cat appeared. Of course, it was a black cat. It was so cliché that I was sure a member of the studio planted it. However, Rosa Lee was certainly not expecting it and pointed at it and said "What the hell is that cat doing in here?"

Before anyone could respond, the cat had knocked over one of the candles, and although it did not catch anything on fire, it spilled a puddle of wax on the Ouija board. To complicate matters, Barry then jumped out of my mother's arms and started to chase the cat all over the stage, knocking various items over as they continued their escapade.

"Stop filming!" Manny announced. "Let's get things cleaned up here." Stop filming? I thought directors were supposed to yell 'Cut!'

Rosa Lee vacated her normally calm and friendly demeanor and screamed. "Where the hell did this cat come from? We can't stop filming. It's a black cat. It may have something to do with Della. This could be a once in a lifetime event that we must capture on film!" She pointed at the cameraman "DO NOT stop filming. Edit it later. DO NOT stop filming!"

"Calm down Rosa!" Manny pleaded. "It will just take a few minutes to straighten out the set. The cat has been hanging around the studio for the past few weeks. It's nothing supernatural. We just can't seem to catch the damn thing."

Barry continued his chase, which had now left the stage and was going up, down and over the seats in the audience area.

My mother had resumed her silent film star shock face and stared directly into the camera again.

"Helen. You can stop now. The camera is off." Suzie scolded her.

Barry continued his pursuit of the cat, now joined by three members of the production crew. None of them were making any headway in capturing the cat.

"Will someone get the dog, please?" Manny asked. "We can't catch the cat if the dog keeps chasing it."

Penny who had been silent since taking her seat stuck two fingers in her mouth, whistled loudly, and then yelled "Come here Barry. Come here boy." So much for "girly" and "giggly!"

Barry's ears pricked up and he stopped for a moment contemplating whether he should obey her command. He then looked back at Penny, cocked his head as if to say "Sorry Penny. This is too much fun", and then continued his pursuit. Penny took off after him continuing to whistle loudly through her fingers.

I provided Daphne and Martin with an update. Daphne suggested, "Della, why don't you catch the damn cat and make it do something unusual? That would be something!"

Penny was finally successful in her capture of Barry and returned him to my mother on stage and then returned to her seat in the audience area. Barry let out soft little growls and groans, letting everyone know he was not pleased with the interruption of a rare game for him of "Chase the Cat."

I concentrated, and managed to take hold of the cat and transport her in the air back towards the front of the stage.

"FOR CHRIST SAKE GET THIS ON FILM!" Rosa Lee screamed.

I floated the cat back and forth across the stage and then deposited it in Penny's lap and the cat purred contentedly.

"That was something but let's try to keep the cat off the stage for now!" Rosa Lee requested. "Let's get this show back on the road before we lose Della!"

"He's just scared." Penny responded, referring to the cat. "I'll keep him right here. Poor little guy!" Penny sat back in her seat and started softly stroking the cat.

I focused in on the cat. He was a cute little fellow. I adored dogs and never really considered myself a cat person, although I liked cats well enough. The cat seemed to stare at me with the most beautiful emerald green eyes which looked remarkably similar to Rosa Lee's. It continued to purr contentedly. Forgetting I was not physically present, I felt myself reaching out to pet the cat. Of course, since I did not have any physical arms, I am not quite sure how I could have experienced such a feeling but that is exactly what it felt like. I could actually feel the softness of its fur, the warmth of its body and the vibration from its purring. It was such a comforting feeling and oddly hypnotizing.

Before I knew what had happened, there was a soft pop sound and I felt my energy merging with the cat. I then felt the strange feeling of being sucked through a funnel I had felt just after my death but it was achingly warm and welcoming. I looked up and gazed directly into Penny's eyes through my new cat eyes. She looked down at me with adoration and said, "You are such a sweet fella... I think I might just take you home!"

Manny called down to Penny. "If you take him home and get him out of our hair, I owe you an expensive dinner with champagne. He has been running around here for weeks and we could never catch him. And look at him, he just adores you!"

Penny answered, "It's a deal. What time are you picking me up?"

Manny smiled a broad grin, "How about right after we finish filming?"

Penny smiled and said "It's a date!"

Meanwhile, Barry, who had not taken his eyes of the cat the whole time, dashed out of my mother's arms directly towards the cat... who was now me... or me, him... or something like that. An instinctive feeling of fear started to penetrate me. Wait a minute... this is Barry. I can't be afraid of Barry!

Penny started to stand up but not before Barry arrived at her seat and jumped quickly up on her lap. Barry's tail was now wagging and he stared into my eyes and then he gave me a big wet kiss right on my furry face. Penny laughed, "I think they like each other!"

To add to the situation, I looked down and licked Barry with my new scratchy little cat tongue right on his nose.

Thirty

Well, there you have it! My death experience thus far. Perhaps, not what you expected? Most certainly not what I expected! However, my life now couldn't be better, or at the very least, it isn't unpleasant, though it could probably be better.

Penny, my best friend, is also now the proud parent of me, a pretty black cat although I never really before thought of myself as pretty. Maybe it is also not the best descriptor anyway, since I am now physically a male. Well, hell, if a woman can be handsome, a male cat can be pretty.

Penny decided to name me "Stuart" which is certainly ironic. I am not sure where she came up with the name as she had no idea of my experiences with my old friend Stuart the energy ball. Perhaps, I provided her with the idea subconsciously. Maybe, she has a Stuart in her family. Possibly, she just loves the name. It is a nice name and Barry, of course, was taken. One can never be sure about this crazy thing we call life or this crazy thing we call death. Penny is also now the permanent guardian of Barry, who is now also my best animal friend.

After several dates, Penny "shacked up" with Manny and we have all moved into his gorgeous apartment in Brooklyn. Penny couldn't be happier. Although they haven't married, as I am not sure Penny is really ready for that again, they are very happy. They have adopted "Ready to Take A Chance Again" by Mr. Manilow as "their song" in my memory, I believe. I have also found out that Penny actually <u>does</u> own a Barry Manilow Christmas CD although she would never have admitted that to me.

I am still able to keep connected to both Martin and Daphne. Daphne is a little shocked that I am content to remain as a cat. What the hell they have nine lives though, right? Martin, of course, thinks it is a pretty cool deal.

Rosa Lee has become an even bigger star, and has a new show with wider distribution that is now on one of the major networks, and Suzie has become one of her frequent advisors on the show as well as a famous psychic in her own right. I get to watch the show sometimes when Penny leaves the television on.

My mother eventually returned to Florida and from what I understand, ended up divorcing Kellin after she found he had been cheating on her with a younger woman. He is lucky she didn't shoot his cojones off. She is a good shot as we now know. She has found a man closer to her own age and from the limited information I have is pretty happy. She did enjoy some fame on the Internet for a while and I am sure video clips of her from Rosa Lee's show are still making their rounds. I know for a fact the Dancing Doll video is still a hit.

I am not sure quite what happened to Cindy Benson, but I certainly wish her the best. I hope she has found some happiness, love, peace, money and is not currently incarcerated. Although I have had no further communication with Janet, I am sure she and my brother continue to be just fine.

I am able to communicate psychically with Barry, and we are closer than any dog and cat you have ever seen. I have since learned that Barry himself has also lived a human existence previously, and is still uncertain as to where his final journey will bring him. Telling his story is a topic for a different day, but let's just say he was a pretty well-known singer and actor, died in the sixties, was from England and you probably still hear some of his songs on your local Easy Listening station. I am pretty sure he and Barry Manilow would have gotten on fabulously.

Although I have not encountered any other possessed dolls to carry on conversations with, I have found as the British doll Catherine had clued me into, the fact that spirits can inhabit any and all things if you can just somehow learn to connect with them. I have had pleasant conversations with a housefly, for example, although I am sure Penny just thought I was mesmerized and looking for a fun meal or new airborne toy.

I also, despite being at least somewhat back in the human realm, am still able to communicate psychically with humans seeking to make contact with the dead. Ironically, if you exclude purring, I can't speak to Penny, Manny or the others humans directly around me although perhaps I could if they held a séance.

I amuse myself for endless hours communicating with psychics and non-psychics alike, telling them stories of my own life and lives I wish I had lived. I seldom tell them they are communicating with a New York cat. I'm not sure why exactly I stretch the truth, as it does make me feel a little guilty at times. Perhaps, I think that although they may truly believe they are communicating with the dead, the prospect of communicating with a living reincarnated cat may be too much for them to swallow. I also feel it is as entertaining for them as it is for me and gives them some hope that there is something beyond death. After all, everyone can use a little hope.

So, if you see your cat lounging in a sunny spot making strange noises, they could actually be involved in a séance with a group of giggling adolescent girls in Missoula, Montana; a psychic in Hot Springs, Arkansas; or they could just simply be lounging in the sun.

Penny does somehow seem to understand many of my needs intuitively, so maybe there is some sort of mental communication between us. As far as I know, she has no clue that her new cat is the most recent incarnation of her old best friend Della. However, I am sure her eyes have opened a little wider to the possibility of life after death. She certainly has a new outlook on love and men. She really loves Manny and I am really, really happy about that.

I am not sure what will happen to me after I leave my current feline incarnation, and I am not sure what happened to the soul of the cat who previously inhabited this body. All I know is I am happy and content, spending my remaining nine lives with my best human friend and my best animal friend.

Some final words of wisdom. Canned cat food really doesn't taste that bad. It is pretty liberating to poop in a litter box and have someone clean all that up for you. Please shut the door if you are involved in romantic interludes, it looks nowhere near as sexy when you are a voyeur. And finally, love those in your life when you can. You never know when you will see them again. Enjoy each moment and rest assured, no one knows what happens after you die. Not even me... Della. And I'm dead...well sort of anyway... whatever dead really means. I am still trying to figure that out.

Made in the USA
Middletown, DE
26 July 2015